THE LIVES
OF THE SAINTS

OMER
ENGLEBERT

THE LIVES
OF THE SAINTS

Translated by
Christopher and Anne Fremantle

penguin books

PENGUIN BOOKS
Published by the Penguin Group
Penguin Books USA Inc., 375 Hudson Street,
New York, New York 10014, U.S.A.
Penguin Books Ltd, 27 Wrights Lane,
London W8 5TZ, England
Penguin Books Australia Ltd, Ringwood,
Victoria, Australia
Penguin Books Canada Ltd, 10 Alcorn Avenue,
Toronto, Ontario, Canada M4V 3B2
Penguin Books (N.Z.) Ltd, 182–190 Wairau Road,
Auckland 10, New Zealand

Penguin Books Ltd, Registered Offices:
Harmondsworth, Middlesex, England

Published in Penguin Books 1995

ISBN 0 14 60.0106 0

Printed in the United States of America

Introductory Note

There is generally too much and too little in Lives of the Saints—too much pious exegesis, too little factual information about the saint. Father Omer Englebert has sought to remedy this excess and this lack, and he is uniquely qualified to do so. For he is not only an historian of impeccable authenticity—his life of Saint Francis is the only Catholic one that can be set beside the great scholarly tome of Paul Sabatier, the most erudite of Protestants—but he is also the editor of a new edition of Migne's *Patrologia*, which is the great source for all our knowledge of the Apostolic and the Desert Fathers.

Omer Englebert was born in the Ardennes, on March 31st, 1893. His father, a local landowner, belonged to a family settled at Ollomont-Nadrin for many centuries. His mother, also of local land-owning stock, had Rhenish and Spanish blood. Until the age of eleven, he lived in a little village hidden in the mountains, chiefly occupied with his two pet goats, his dog and his tame crow. He studied at the Ecclesiastical College of Battogne. A bad pupil, he cared only for music and history.

He wished to become a Franciscan, but his health would not permit it. So he became a secular priest, being ordained *propter beneficia*, and thus being under the jurisdiction of no bishop. This suited his itinerant temperament, and his travels have taken him over all Europe except Russia, and to both North and South America.

In 1919 he founded a monthly, *La Terre Wallonne*. Ordained in 1924 by Cardinal Mercier, he was made by him literary editor of *Vingtieme Siècle*. His first book, *La Sagesse du Curé Pecquet*, appeared in 1927, and was an immediate and lasting success. It has been translated into most of the European languages, and was followed by two later volumes, *Le Curé Pecquet Continue* and *Le Curé Pecquet Vit Encore*. Of this character, Henri Clouard writes in his *Histoire de la Littérature Française:* "Essentially true to type, this Father Pecquet is one of the few real priests in modern literature. He gives to orthodoxy the savour of paradox, and defends divine government with all the brilliance usually reserved to the opposition. Moreover the remarks of this saintly individual reflect a wisdom which is marvellously, fully, and sweetly profane."

Henri Clouard sums up the author of the Curé Pequet books, of *Vie et Conversion d'Ève Lavallièrre, Le Père Damien Apôtre des Lépreux, Vie de Saint Martin, Vie de Saint Pascal Baylon*, and numerous other books by saying, "What distinguishes him is a robust and realistic spirit exacting in substantial values, and therefore opposed to all that is confused, and superficial, in psychology, morals and politics."

—Anne Fremantle

St. Agatha (d. 251)
February 5th

We do not possess any entirely reliable information about this martyr, who has been honoured since the most ancient times and whose name has been included in the canon of the Mass.

Two cities in Sicily, Catania and Palermo, dispute the honour of her birth. Young, beautiful, and rich, Agatha lived from childhood a life entirely consecrated to God.

In betrayal of the duties of his office, a greedy and shameless magistrate named Quinctianus profited by Decius' edicts of persecution to attempt to abuse the virgin and to steal her fortune. He first delivered her to a matron charged with perverting her, who, however, failed. Then he made her appear before him on three occasions. The first time she was slapped in the face for having repelled the judge's solicitations and affirmed her faith. The second, Quinctianus had her stretched on a wooden horse; the executioner tipped her flesh with iron hooks and was ordered to cut off her breasts. Agatha then said to the brutal magistrate: "Cruel man, have you forgotten your mother and the breast that nourished you, that you dare to mutilate me in such a way?"

The third interrogation had no more success in changing her constancy. Fresh tortures were inflicted on her by rolling her, naked, on burning coals. Then a violent earthquake shook the town of Catania; a piece of wall broke off, crushing the judge's assessor who was his friend; the judge himself fled, terrified. As for Agatha, having thanked God for his help, she gave a great cry and expired.

I

St. Agnes (d. middle or end of the 3rd century)
JANUARY 21ST

We possess little reliable data on this very celebrated saint. Some place her martyrdom about 254; others under Diocletian, about 304.

Agnes was twelve when she was faced with sacrificing to the gods and renouncing her virginity. Neither threats nor promises could turn her. She was tortured. Those watching her torment wept. She, on the contrary, continued to appear happy. Several young men presented themselves, who wished to marry her. "It is an insult to my heavenly Spouse," she said, "to try to please me. He shall have me for His own, who first chose me. Why, executioner, all this delay? May this body perish rather than delight the eyes of those that I refuse."

According to the Latin tradition, Agnes was beheaded. According to the Greek tradition she was first sent into a house of ill repute, where her virtue was miraculously preserved; then she was thrown on to a pyre.

St. Anne (1st century)
JULY 26TH

The name of the mother of Our Lady is known to us only through tradition; the Holy Scriptures do not in fact mention St. Anne at all; on the other hand the apocryphal gospels speak of her abundantly. *The Protevangelium of James* tells us that she was, like Joachim her husband, of the tribe of Juda, that both led a saintly life, possessed great herds, but unfortunately had no children. Among the Jews this was the worst ignominy; for Joachim it meant that at times the offering he brought to the temple was refused. But the day came when, after many prayers and humiliations, Anne gave birth to Mary, most perfect of human creatures, who was in turn to give birth to the Saviour.

The cult of St. Anne spread at first in the East; in the year 550 the Emperor Justinian raised a basilica in her honour at Constantinople; today the Greeks still have not less than three annual feasts to honour the grandmother of Our Lord.

In the West devotion to St. Anne seems to have gained popularity at the time of the crusades. Her feast, suppressed by St. Pius V, was re-established by Gregory XIII in 1594; Gregory XV in 1622 ordained it a public holiday; since Leo XIII it is celebrated in the Latin Church as a rite of the second class.

Nowhere in the world is St. Anne honoured and invoked as in Brittany where, from 1623 to 1625, she appeared to Yves Nicolazic de Keranna near Auray.

St. Anselm (d. 1109)
APRIL 21ST

Anselm was born at Aosta in Piedmont about 1033. Gundulf, his father, was related to Countess Mathilda; Ermenberga, his mother, was thought to be descended from the founder of the dynasty of Savoy.

After a childhood devoted to study and piety, Anselm wished to embrace the religious life but Gundulf prevented this and brought him out into the world. The young man acquired a taste for pleasure and devoted several years to it. Meanwhile, Ermenberga died; the father and son quarrelled, and Anselm fled from his father's castle.

With a donkey carrying his baggage, he crossed Mount Cenis where he thought he would die of hunger. He stayed some time in Burgundy, passed three years in France, then became a monk at the abbey of Bec in Normandy, where flourished one of the most celebrated schools in the West and where the famed Lanfranc was a teacher. Anselm was his pupil and afterwards his successor.

He became abbot of the monastery in 1078, and his reputation for learning and goodness quickly spread throughout Europe. "The good odour of your virtues has reached us here," Gregory VII wrote to him. "Come as soon as possible to see us," Urban II bade him for his part, "so that we may together enjoy the affection which unites us." As he felt the approach of death, William the Conqueror had recourse to the ministry of Anselm.

The interests of his abbey sometimes took Anselm to England. In 1092 he was constrained by King William Rufus to remain, and the next year to accept the episcopal see of Canterbury. From then on he had to undertake frequent journeys to Rome to settle the conflicts which incessantly arose between the English court and the Holy See. It is surprising that in the midst of such diplomatic and administrative labours he was able to compose writings so numerous and so profound.

St. Anselm is considered, in fact, to be one of the great philosophers and theologians of the middle ages. He is also the author of some admirable prayers. Alexander VI canonized him in 1492 and in 1720 Clement XI placed him among the ranks of Doctors of the Church.

St. Anthony of the Desert (d. 356)
JANUARY 17TH

Born in 250, near Heracleus in Upper Egypt, Anthony lost his parents at the age of about twenty. His first action was to complete his sister's education; then he sold the house, furniture, and hundred acres of land which he possessed, giving the proceeds to the poor, and joined the anchorites who lived in the neighbourhood. He retired into an empty sepulchre, where at once began those struggles with the demon which he had to support throughout his life.

At the age of thirty-five he plunged into the desert alone. For twenty years he lived in an abandoned fort, the entrance to which he had barricaded, but his admirers finally broke in. Anthony then miraculously cured several sick people and consented to give spiritual counsel to some souls. His special recommendation to them was to base their rule of life on the Gospel. Little by little so many disciples came that he was able to found two monasteries, one on the right bank of the Nile at Pispir, the other on the left bank beside Arsinoe.

Anthony appeared for a few days at Alexandria in 311, to fight the Arian heresy and to comfort the victims of Maximinus' persecution. Before his death he had the joy of seeing his sister once more. She also had grown old in the search for perfection and directed a community of dedicated virgins. Filled with serenity, he ended his existence at the age of a hundred and five in a cave on Mount Colzim.

This great ascetic was always perfectly modest and courteous. He has been called the "father of cenobites", because it was in great part due to him that the monastic life spread in the East and later in the West. In addition, he inspired innumerable souls by his example and

5

maxims, His *Life*, written by St. Athanasius, had an immense influence both on art and hagiography.

St. Anthony of Padua (1195-1231)
JUNE 13TH

Born at Lisbon in 1195, Anthony was canon regular at Holy Cross at Coimbra when, in 1220, the remains of the first Franciscan martyrs were brought back from Morocco to be buried in his church. Burning to follow in the footsteps of these heroes, he left his order to enter that of the Friars Minor and set out for Morocco; but he almost immediately fell sick, re-embarked, and was thrown by a storm on to the Sicilian coast. There he joined some brothers from Messina who were going to the Portiuncula, to the general chapter of 1221. Nobody at the Portiuncula bothered about him; and they would have even forgotten to make any provision for him but for the intervention of Brother Gratian, provincial of Lombardy, who agreed to take him under his charge. Anthony lived from that time on in a cave at the hermitage of San Paolo, near Forli, leaving it only to attend holy office and to sweep the monastery. But his theological knowledge and rhetorical talents were revealed one day of ordination at Forli, when an expected preacher failed them and his brethren obliged him to speak impromptu. From then on, except for time set aside for instruction which he gave at Bologna, Toulouse, and Montpellier, he preached until the end of his life, sometimes in Lombardy where he fought the Cathari with great resource of learning; again in France where his journeys to Brive, Arles, Bourges, and Limoges are remembered; again in Padua where he died at the height of his fame, aged thirty-six. He was canonized less than a year after his death. This remarkable orator spoke every tongue, it is said, and the *Fioretti* assures us that even the fish listened to him in delight.

St. Anthony of Padua is without doubt the most popular wonder-worker of the Latin Church; his devotees and his statues are found everywhere; he is invoked in every need; St. Francis de Sales asserted that he had the power of finding lost articles; Pius XII declared him doctor of the Church on January 16th, 1946.

St. Augustine (354-430)
AUGUST 28TH

Aurelius Augustinus was born at Tagaste in Numidia on November 13th, 354. His father, Patricius, a pagan of moderate means, was baptized on his deathbed; his mother was St. Monica, of whom we have spoken on May 4th. She had her son inscribed among the catechumens and instructed him in the elements of Christianity. But Augustine lost his faith in the course of the studies he pursued from 365 to 369 at Madaurus, and from 370 to 374 at Carthage. From the age of sixteen he was given to sensuality, and about 372 formed a liaison with the woman who for a dozen years he regarded as his wife, and by whom he had a son named Adeodatus.

From 375 to 383 Augustine taught rhetoric at Carthage, and from 383 to 385 at Milan. There he broke with the Manichaeans, who for nine years had considered him as one of themselves. He found his faith again in 386 and was baptized with Adeodatus by St. Ambrose at the end of Lent of the following year.

In the autumn of 387 Augustine was at Ostia, ready to return to Africa with his mother, but she died unexpectedly; he stayed at Rome for a year and only went back to Tagaste at the end of 388. He at once distributed his goods to the poor and founded a monastery in one of his former estates. Moreover, until his death he himself led the monastic life.

Augustine became a priest of the church of Hippo at the beginning of 391, and he was at first charged with the preaching ministry. In 395, Bishop Valerius took him as coadjutor and the following year Augustine replaced him. He died on August 28th, 430, while the Vandals were besieging his episcopal city, in the midst of the fall of the Roman Empire.

St. Augustine is generally held to be the greatest doctor of Christianity. Of his ninety-six works the greater part are held as authoritative by all the Christian churches; certain, like the *Confessions* and the *City of God*, are known to all educated people. Some of his writings are refutations of Manichaeism, Donatism, Pelagianism, and other heresies of his time; others deal with spirituality, philosophy, history, exegesis, and morals. He preached innumerable sermons, of which more than four hundred have come down to us. We also have extant two hundred and seventeen of his letters.

St. Barbara (d. about 235)
DECEMBER 4TH

The *Acts* of St. Barbara are of a doubtful era and little worthy of credence. It would seem that her martyrdom took place at Nicomedia, under Maximinus of Thrace, whose persecution only lasted three years but was in certain places extremely cruel. This former prize-fighter, built like Hercules, who drank an amphora of wine a day and amused himself by breaking horses' jawbones with one blow of his fist, had Alexander Severus, his predecessor, assassinated; he persecuted the Christians, Eusebius tells us, for the sole reason that Alexander had left them in peace; and he was completely indifferent to the fact that his orders were executed with the most barbarous refinements.

The romantic author of the *Acts* tells us that Barbara was placed by her father Dioscorus in a palace topped with a high tower and surrounded by marvellous gardens. There she received philosophers, orators, and poets, appointed to teach her the secrets of all things. The only result of their lessons was to make her see the absurdity of polytheism. Origen, whom she consulted, sent her his disciple Valentinian, who taught her the mysteries of Christianity and secretly baptized her. Barbara then resolved to remain a virgin and to dedicate herself entirely to God. She threw out of the window the statues of the false gods which filled her palace, traced the sign of the cross over almost all the walls, and to the two openings which were pierced in the high tower she added a third in honour of the Blessed Trinity.

For Dioscorus these were all horrible sacrileges, worthy of death. He drew his sword to strike the blasphemer, but she fled to the mountains. He caught up with her and dragged her home by her hair; then he handed her over to the prefect Marcian, to whom Maximinus had confided the suppression of Christianity in that neighbourhood. On Marcian's orders, Barbara was beaten with rods, torn with iron hooks, and suffered other torments; then, since an end had to be made, her father asked for the honour of dispatching her. Dioscorus led his daughter out of town and cut off her head with a blow from an axe.

9

St. Bartholomew (1st century)
AUGUST 24TH

In the list of apostles given in the Synoptic Gospels and the Acts, the name of Bartholomew is always joined with that of Philip; from this it has been concluded that the two were old friends. But apart from his title of "apostle," no other details about St. Bartholomew are given us in these passages of the Scripture.

St. John does not mention him in listing, albeit incompletely, the apostolic college. Twice, however, he speaks of a friend of Philip called Nathanael, who was "of the disciples" of the Saviour.

Had Bartholomew two names? Is he the same person as Nathanael? In this case the following passage from the fourth Gospel tells us the circumstances in which he became a member of the apostolic college:

We are at the banks of the Jordan where on seeing Jesus St. John the Baptist cries: "Look, this is the Lamb of God; look, this is he who takes away the sin of the world." Three of his own disciples, John, Andrew, and Simon, leave him to join Our Lord from then on. "He was to remove into Galilee next day; and now he found Philip; to him Jesus said, Follow me ... And Philip found Nathanael, and told him, We have discovered who it was Moses wrote of in his law, and the prophets too; it is Jesus the son of Joseph, from Nazareth. When Nathanael asked him, Can anything that is good come from Nazareth? Philip said, Come and see. Jesus saw Nathanael coming towards him, and said of him, Here comes one who belongs to the true Israel; there is no falsehood in him. How dost thou know me? Nathanael asked; and Jesus answered him, I saw thee when thou wast under the fig-tree, before Philip called thee. Then Nathanael answered him, Thou, Master, art the Son of God, thou art the King of Israel. Jesus answered, What, believe because I told thee that I saw thee under the fig-tree? Thou shalt see greater things than that. And he said to him, Believe me when I tell you this; you will see heaven opening, and the angels of God going up and coming down upon the Son of Man" (John i, 29-51).

St. John again mentions Nathanael in the passage where he shows the risen Jesus appearing on the shore of the Lake of Tiberias, eating a repast of bread and fish with His disciples (John xxi, 1-15).

Towards the end of the 4th century, Rufinus affirms that Bartholomew had preached the Gospel "in nearer India," but this is a late and vague indication; and we have no other on the life which St. Bartholomew led after the dispersal of the apostolic college.

St. Bede the Venerable (673-735)
MAY 27TH

The Venerable Bede was born at the time of the completion of the conversion of England begun about the year 600, as is well known, by St. Augustine of Canterbury. He himself, shortly before his death, outlined his life in the epilogue of his English history.

"I, Bede, servant of Christ and priest of the abbey of St. Peter and St. Paul at Wearmouth and Jarrow, have compiled this history, with the help of God, using for it old documents, ancient traditions, and what I have been able to see with my own eyes. Born in the neighbourhood of the said monastery, I was only seven years old when my parents confided me to the care of the Abbot Benedict (Biscop). Since then I have passed my whole life in the cloister, dividing my time between study of Holy Writ, regular observance and daily celebration of the Holy Office. My whole happiness was in studying, teaching, and writing. I was ordained deacon at nineteen, and priest at thirty, these two orders being conferred on me by Bishop John of Beverley. Since I became priest till the present time, when I have reached the age of fifty-nine, I have employed my time in writing, for my own use and that of my brothers, commentaries on Holy Scripture, sometimes taken from the Holy Fathers, sometimes conceived in their spirit and according to their interpretation."

Setting out a list of his works, he enumerates forty-five, some of which have been lost. Some treat of figures of rhetoric, cosmography, orthography, and even of thunder. The greater part are those works of exegesis which he has mentioned. In introducing into his country the patristic riches of former centuries, Bede did for England what Cassiodorus, Gregory of Tours, and St. Isidore did respectively for Italy, France, and Spain. His poems no longer exist. Among his letters, there are some which are veritable treatises. As for his *Ecclesiastical History of the English People*, which covers the period from their origins to 731, it is unanimously considered to be excellent, and to historians it is indispensable.

St. Benedict (d. 543)
MARCH 21ST

Born at Norcia in Umbria about 480, Benedict was pious and virtuous from childhood. He studied in Rome and the sight of the disorderliness of his fellow students made him fear to fall, in his turn, into sin; without taking leave of anyone, he fled to the mountains of Subiaco.

There a monk named Romanus gave him the religious habit and

showed him as a place of retreat a cave known to none. Benedict had lived there for three years when the fame of his virtues reached some monks whose abbot had just died. They insisted that Benedict become his successor, but certain of them, finding him too severe, put poison in his wine. The glass broke when Benedict, according to his custom, traced the sign of the cross over his drink. "I have often warned you," he said, getting up, "that we would never suit each other." And he returned to his cave. However, more and more disciples placed themselves under his guidance. He built twelve monasteries for them, each of twelve monks, at the head of which was an abbot.

About 529, Benedict left Subiaco with Maurus, Placidus, and some others and turned towards Monte Cassino. There stood altars dedicated to Venus, Jupiter, and Apollo. The holy man broke the idols, upset the altars, set fire to the sacred grove, and in spite of all the persecutions of the demon built an abbey which has since been many times destroyed but which has always risen from its ashes.

The rule which was observed there, founded on silence, work, prayer, contrition of heart, and respect for the human person, is a monument of wisdom that has survived the centuries. There was a time when forty thousand monasteries followed it in the West.

A few weeks after the death of his sister Scholastica, Benedict had her tomb opened as he wished to be laid to rest beside her. He was then without warning taken with a violent fever. The sixth day he was carried at his wish into the oratory of St. John the Baptist and there received the viaticum; then, standing with his hands lifted to heaven, he drew his last breath.

St. Bernadette (1844–1879)
APRIL 16TH

The celebrated confidante of Mary Immaculate was born at Lourdes on January 7th, 1844. François Soubirous and Louise Casterot, her parents, were very poor, and the child was put into service from the age of twelve to fourteen. She came back to her family at the beginning of the 1858 to prepare for her first Communion. Some days afterwards, as she was collecting firewood with her sister and a friend, the Blessed Virgin appeared in the crevasse of a rock on the bank of the Gave. This apparition took place on February 11th.

Clad in a white robe, girdled with a blue sash, a white veil covering her head, her bare feet ornamented with a golden rose, a rosary hanging from her right hand, Our Lady seemed to be sixteen or seventeen. She returned eighteen times before the following July 16th. She entered into conversations with the little girl and, among other things, said to her: "I promise to make you happy, if not in this world, at least in the next (February 18th). Pray for poor sinners (February 21st). Penance! Penance! (February 24th). Go and tell the priests that a chapel should be built here (February 27th). I am the Immaculate Conception (March 25th)."

The sisters of Nevers had a house at Lourdes where they cared for the sick and instructed children. They received Bernadette, taught her to read and write, completed her religious instruction, kept her busy with light work until the day when, aged twenty-two, she was admitted as a sick and indigent person into their congregation.

Bernadette left for Nevers in July 1866 to commence her novitiate at the motherhouse. There she passed the rest of her life, employed at one time as infirmarian, at another as sacristan; usually ailing, often in bed, constantly humiliated and even a little persecuted by her superiors. She always suffered with courage and sought to be despised. In her agony she was heard to murmur: "Holy Mary, mother of God, pray for me, poor sinner, poor sinner." A few instants later she softly drew her last breath.

St. Bernard of Clairvaux (1090–1153)
AUGUST 20TH

Immense was the influence wielded by St. Bernard on the spirituality of the West. This influence appears in such later writings as *The Imitation of Christ*, which follows his doctrine and sometimes his very words.

He was born of a noble family at Fontaines-les-Dijon in 1090. After a virtuous youth, he became at twenty-two a monk of the abbey of Cîteaux, taking with him four of his brothers, twenty-five of his friends, and his uncle Gaudry. His father, Tescelin, and his youngest brother, Nicard, joined them a few years later.

Bernard then governed the monastery of Clairvaux, which he had founded in 1115 and which soon was to number as many as seven hundred monks. Clairvaux spread in its turn and gave birth, even in the lifetime of its founder, to one hundred and sixty daughter houses. The religious activities of Bernard were by no means limited to houses of the Cistercian reform; they extended to the clergy, the order of the Templars, and even to the Benedictines of Cluny who, however, would never consent to his wish to banish works of art from their churches.

His activity was extended everywhere. It fell to him to remind the kings of France, Louis the Fat and Louis the Young, of their duties; he made the celebrated Abelard and Gilbert de la Porrée retract or suffer condemnation when their errors or theological subtleties threatened to imperil dogma. He thrice crossed the Alps to put an end to the schism of the anti-Pope Anacletus II; preached at Vézelay; crossed the Rhineland; wrote on many subjects; moved all of Europe to organize the second crusade, the failure of which was so painful to him. With the object of reforming the Roman Curia which was attacked by Arnold of Brescia, he composed the *De Consideratone*, intended for Pope Eugene III, a former monk of Clairvaux and his disciple.

There have come down to us from St. Bernard some ten other spiritual treatises, more than three hundred sermons, and more than five hundred letters. A host of writings have been attributed to him, such as the *Memorare*, the *Ave Maris Stella*, and the *Salve Regina*, which are not his.

St. Blaise (d. about 316)
FEBRUARY 3RD

This is what is told of the great healer in his *Acts* of martyrdom which, however, are somewhat legendary:

Blaise was born in Armenia and devoted himself to medicine until his election to the episcopal see of Sebaste. This dignity, however, did not prevent him from withdrawing to a cave on Mount Argeus, which he made his habitual residence. There, as is shown in the window in Notre Dame at Chartres, the sick came in crowds to consult him, and not only men but animals as well. He cured them and sent them away with his blessing. A strange thing was that the animals never disturbed him at prayer, however great their need.

Under the Emperor Licinius, Agricola, governor of Cappadocia, came to Sebaste and persecuted the Christians. In quest of wild beasts for the games in the arena, they sent hunters out to beat through the neighbouring woods. These hunters, passing near the cave on Mount Argeus, saw wolves, tigers, bears, and lions waiting for Blaise to finish his prayers. The saint was thus discovered. Agricola ordered his arrest and attempted to make him apostasize. Several such attempts on his part brought only humiliating replies from the saint.

Between interrogations Blaise was returned to prison. Here the unfortunate still managed to reach him. He gave a poor woman back her pig which a wolf had stolen. He also cured a little girl who, in eating fish, had swallowed a bone and was choking. From this came the habit of invoking St. Blaise for maladies of the throat. There also came to those who, as though choked in the confessional, did not dare to confess their sins. He is also considered as the protector and healer of animals.

After enduring various torments, Blaise was thrown into a lake. He walked upon the water and invited his persecutors to join him there. They could thus show, he said, the power of the gods they were urging him to honour. The pagans took up the challenge and were drowned to the last man. Blaise was then told by an angel to return to dry land to receive martyrdom, and he was beheaded on the shore.

St. Bridget (d. 1373)
OCTOBER 8TH

Bridget was born about 1302 at Finsta Castle near Uppsala. When she was fourteen she married Ulf of Nericia, a prince of the blood, by whom she had eight children. Some of them lived rather wickedly; others embraced the religious life; Catherine, the saint's daughter and wonted companion, merited canonization.

Bridget at one time was governess to the young wife of Magnus, king of Sweden. When she saw that she could do this flighty person no good, she left the court and went on a pilgrimage with her husband. In 1341 they visited Cologne, Tarascon, Sainte-Baume, and St. James in Galicia. At Arras, on their return journey, Prince Ulf first had attacks of the malady from which he was to die three years later. Before he died he placed on his wife's finger a gold ring which he asked her to keep as a token of their mutual and undying love.

Widowed, Bridget pursued afresh her taste for penance and contemplation. To worldly people who mocked her way of life she replied: "It was not on your account that I began, and your mockeries will not prevent my continuing." God favoured her with great graces, and the *Revelations* which she has left on the passion of the Saviour are very well known. Before leaving Sweden to settle in Rome, she had founded a congregation of nuns at Vadstena, of which her daughter, Catherine, became superior. It spread as far as Spain and later to Mexico.

From 1350 to 1364, St. Bridget and St. Catherine lived together in Rome; from 1364 to 1367 they made a pilgrimage to Assisi, Monte

Gargano, Bari, Benevento, and Naples; in 1371 they made a journey to the Holy Land.

Bridget was many times inspired to recall kings and clergy to their duties. Popes Clement VI, Urban V, and Gregory XI venerated her and had recourse to her counsel. Constantly she pressed them to leave Avignon in order to return to Rome.

Her last years were full of trials and temptations; but finally her heart regained the sense of God's presence, and she died in ecstasy. First interred in Rome in the church of the Poor Clares of Viminal, her body afterwards was returned to Sweden and placed in the convent of Vadstena.

St. Cecilia (period unknown)
NOVEMBER 22ND

We still may see in the cypress-wood coffin at Trastevere the beheaded body of St. Cecilia, wearing the robe of cloth of gold in which the virgin was dressed when she was taken to the catacombs. But the story of her martyrdom is full of doubtful details. We do not even know at what epoch she lived; some make her a contemporary of Marcus Aurelius, others a victim of the persecution of Diocletian or that of Julian the Apostate.

She was, it is said, a very cultivated young patrician whose ancestors were illustrious in Rome's history. Although she had vowed her virginity to God, her parents married her to Valerian, who lived at Trastevere. "O *dulcissime et amantissime juvenis*—O very sweet and very loving youth," said Cecilia to him after the wedding ceremony, "there is a mystery which I will confide to you if you swear to guard it faithfully." He swore to do so. She then revealed to him that an angel watched over her. "But in order to see him," she added, "you must first be purified."

On her advice Valerian went to find old Urban, who lived in hiding among the Christian tombs, and received baptism from him. On returning, he found Cecilia at prayer and an angel at her side. The latter, who held in his hand two crowns, placed one on Cecilia's brow, the other on Valerian's, and in addition he offered the latter to grant him a favour. All that Valerian asked was that the grace of baptism should also be given to his brother Tiburtius.

As the persecution became more rigorous, and the two brothers undertook to inter the faithful to whom the imperial police refused burial, they were arrested and decapitated. Cecilia was in her turn apprehended for having interred their bodies at her villa on the Appian Way. She was given no alternative but to sacrifice to the gods or to die. She chose death. To the perfect Almachius, who recalled to her that he had the power of life or death over her, she answered: "It is untrue; for if you can give death, you cannot give life." Almachius had condemned her to die by suffocation; but this torture not succeeding, he had her beheaded.

The *Acts* of St. Cecilia contain the following passage: "While the profane music of her wedding was heard, Cecilia was singing in her heart a hymn of love for Jesus, her true spouse." It is this phrase, read without due attention, which aroused belief in the musical talent of St. Cecilia, and has made her the patron saint of musicians.

St. Clare (d. 1253)
AUGUST 12TH

St. Clare, better than anyone else and almost as well as he himself, realized the ideal of St. Francis of Assisi.

Born in that town in 1193 or 1194, she belonged to the noble family of the Offreducci of Coccorano. Her father Faverone died young; her mother Ortolana, as well as her sisters, Agnes and Beatrice, entered the Order of Poor Ladies. This had been founded on the night of Palm Sunday, 1212, when Clare, who had fled from her mother's palace with her cousin Pacifica, joined Francis at the Portiuncula. After having cut off their hair, the Poverello clothed them in coarse brown wool and received their religious profession. The new-born community established itself at San Damiano and from there spread throughout the whole of Europe. Everywhere the Franciscans established themselves went also the daughters of Clare, practising penance, cultivating spiritual joy, and observing poverty as St. Francis wished them to do; that is, deprived of all revenues and depending solely on alms. Today there are still twelve thousand persons leading this kind of existence, which at that time was an innovation in the Church.

Clare loved music and well-composed sermons; she was humble, merciful, charming, optimistic, and chivalrous. She blessed the Creator for having made the world so beautiful; she got up at night to tuck in the bedclothes of her companions who were uncovered; every day from midday to nones, she meditated on the Passion and experienced mysterious tortures which filled her eyes with blood and tears. Learning in 1221 of the martyrdom of the Franciscans in Morocco, she would have gone to the Saracen country to shed her blood if she had not been prevented.

Francis always watched over his "little spiritual plant"; he even wished to console her after his death. The day when his body was being carried to the Church of St. George, the funeral cortège turned aside in order to pass San Damiano. The open bier was borne into the chapel of the recluses; thus Clare could see once more the face of her beloved father. She washed with tears the blessed remains and covered the sacred stigmata with kisses. When twenty-six years later, Clare in her turn was near death, she was heard to murmur: "Depart in peace, for the road thou hast followed is the good one." A sister asked her to whom she was speaking. "I am speaking to my departing soul," she replied, "and he who was its guide is not far away." Doubtless it was St. Francis who was coming to lead her to heaven. "Lord God," she said again, "be blessed for having created me." Then she gave up her spirit.

St. Dorothea (1347-1394)
OCTOBER 30TH

A contemporary of Bridget of Sweden and of Catherine of Siena, Dorothea Swartz was, like them, favoured with ecstasies and visions and has left numerous revelations.

She was born at Montau, near Marienburg, of a family of peasants who had nine children. Marienburg, like Danzig and Marienwerder, where Dorothea later lived, belonged to the Teutonic Knights, then at the height of their power. She lived somewhat under their obedience and jurisdiction, and it was they who, in 1404, introduced the process of her canonization at the court of Rome.

Married to a Danzig workman named Adalbert, Dorothea gave birth to nine children of whom only one daughter survived and became a Benedictine. Her conjugal life was rather difficult. Adalbert, irascible and stupid, was often brutal to his wife; however, they went on long pilgrimages together. In 1389, Dorothea left for Rome alone, in order to arrive for the jubilee the following year. She travelled under the guidance of God, begging her bread, scarcely seeing the countries she traversed. At Rome she fell ill and was cared for, during many weeks, at the hospital of Maria Auxiliatrix. Her husband had been dead some months when she reached home. Then she was able to think about the realization of her old dream of entering religion. For two years she was on probation, after which, on May 2nd, 1393, she was immured in a cell built into the cathedral of Marienwerder. It was a square hole, six feet wide and nine feet high, pierced by three windows, one giving on to the sky; another on to the altar where she took her Communion; the third, on to a cemetery, through which her food was brought. It was in this kind of tomb that Dorothea received the innumerable visits and heavenly communications which her confessors have related. She died there, racked with sufferings and austerities, at the end of a year, June 25th, 1394.

A whole literature has been dedicated to the visionary of Marienwerder; numerous miracles were attributed to her; and the Prussians have chosen her as their patron.

St. Francis of Assisi (d. 1226)
OCTOBER 4TH

Born at Assisi in 1181 or 1182, the son of a rich cloth merchant, Francis Bernardone spent a very flighty youth, taking part in street battles and military adventures. After long months of captivity in the jails of Perugia, divine grace transformed him.

The Gospels, understood literally, became his rule of life, and his only thought was the imitation of Our Lord in all things. Having wedded Lady Poverty, as he expressed it, he was to be seen barefoot, in rough clothes, begging at the gates and preaching purity of heart and peace to all.

A few disciples joined him in 1209. They formed the nucleus of the order of Friars Minor. In 1212, Clare of Assisi placed herself under his guidance and brought into being the order of Sisters of the Poor. The third order was established some ten years later, for people in the world who wished to live the religious life without forsaking their calling.

The *Poverello* made three attempts to visit the Saracens; only one, in 1219, succeeded. Apart from these journeys and some pilgrimages to Rome, he rarely left Umbria.

Francis loved God with an infinite love and all creatures for love of Him. He composed sublime songs to the glory of his brother the Sun, lived on intimate terms with the wolves and the birds, worked with his hands, swept out churches, cared for lepers, and sent food to brigands with his affectionate greetings.

From 1221, displaced by reformers, he resigned the direction of his order; in September 1224 he received the stigmata on Mount Alvernia; on October 3rd, 1226, he lay down naked on the bare earth at the Portiuncula and, singing, received the visit of his sister, Death.

The religious and artistic influence of the *Poverello* was immense and it endures to this day. No other figure has been the subject of so much contemporary literature; he is the saint best beloved of heretics and of sinners. It seems that this is due to his chivalrous character, his absence of book knowledge, his poetic gifts, his charm and, to quote Benedict XV, "because he is the most perfect image of Christ that ever was."

St. Francis de Sales (d. 1622)
JANUARY 29TH

Francis de Sales was born of an old family of Savoy at the Château of Thorens in 1566 or 1567. He began his studies at La Roche and Annecy; he continued them from 1581 to 1588 at Clermont College in Paris; he completed them at the University of Padua in 1591.

In obedience to his father he became, in 1591, an advocate in the senate of Savoy. The following year, free at last to follow his true vocation, he became a priest, and at once began the ministry of preaching and spiritual direction in which he was to display such mastery. From 1594 to 1598 he strove to convert the Protestants of the Chablais and met with success.

He was appointed bishop of Geneva in 1603. From then on his renown travelled beyond the frontiers of the Duchy of Savoy. At Paris, where he preached with success, he became friends with St. Vincent de Paul and directed Madame Acarie and Mother Angélique Arnauld. Henry IV said: "The bishop of Geneva has all the virtues and not a single fault." He proposed to give him a fine and famous French bishopric, but Francis refused. "Sire," he replied, "I am married; my wife is a poor woman, I cannot leave her for a richer one."

In the course of preaching Lent at Dijon, in 1603, he met Madame de Chantal, with whom seven years later he founded the Order of the Visitation.

St. Francis de Sales was a great correspondent. His *Introduction to the Devout Life* is only a compilation of the notes and letters addressed by him to Madame de Charmoisy. When this work appeared, the general of the Carthusians begged him never again to publish anything, fearing that he might be disappointed. But when, in 1614, there appeared the *Treatise on the Love of God*, the same adviser begged him never to stop writing.

Francis died in his fifty-sixth year with the calm which he had always shown. He was counselled to repeat the words of St. Martin: "Lord, if I am still necessary to your people, I do not refuse the labour." He replied: "I, necessary! No, no, I am but a useless servant!" And he thrice repeated the word "useless".

St. Francis Xavier (1506-1552)
DECEMBER 3RD

Professor of philosophy at the University of Paris, Francis Xavier met Ignatius Loyola there and joined the nascent Society of Jesus. On August 15th, 1534, in the church of Montmartre, Ignatius and his companions vowed to leave at the end of a year for the Holy Land. But the war between the venetians and the Turks prevented this, and the pope detailed them to other tasks. For his part, Francis Xavier exercised his zeal for some time at Padua, Bologna, and Rome. Then he went to Portugal, embarked for India with two colleagues, and arrived at Goa on May 6th, 1542.

His missionary activity lasted ten years, during which he covered immense distances, accomplished all sorts of miracles, founded churches and colleges, and achieved apostolic successes which have become a legend. His biographers relate that he baptized not less than forty thousand Palawars; that in the kingdom of Travancore, as later in Japan, he was granted the gift of tongues; that he raised several people from the dead, calmed tempests, often foretold the future, and healed countless persons. It has even been said that he converted a million souls. The history of the missions surely has few pages so glorious.

In 1549, Francis Xavier arrived in Japan, where his travels were no less fecund than in India; he stayed there twenty-eight months, after which he returned to Goa and, on April 14th, 1552, he embarked for China. His dream of evangelizing that country was never realized; the apostle fell ill on the island of Sancian, within sight of Canton. He would have died abandoned on the shore had not a poor man, named George Alvarez, rescued him and carried him to his hut. There he drew his last breath, December 2nd, 1552.

St. Gabriel, Archangel
MARCH 24TH

St. Gabriel, with St. Michael and St. Raphael, is one of the three archangels designated by name in Holy Scripture. The four episodes in which he is mentioned are connected with the mystery of the Incarnation.

Twice he came to explain to the prophet Daniel the meaning of certain visions relative to the coming of the Messias (Daniel viii, 16-26; ix, 21).

Later, at the dawn of a new epoch, he appeared to the priest Zachary in the temple at Jerusalem "at the hour of sacrifice . . . standing at the right of the altar where incense was burnt." It was to announce to him that his wife, advanced in age, would give birth to a son who would be the Precursor of the Saviour. As Zachary remained incredulous, he said to him: "My name is Gabriel, and my place is in God's presence; I have been sent to speak with thee, and to bring thee this good news. Behold, thou shalt be dumb, and have no power of speech, until the day when this is accomplished; and that, because thou hast not believed my promise" (Luke i, 11-20).

The third mission of this ambassador from heaven is that which he fulfilled to the Virgin Mary:

"Hail, thou who art full of grace," he said as he entered the house at Nazareth; "the Lord is with thee; blessed art thou among women. . . . Thou shalt bear a son and shalt call him Jesus. He shall be great and men will know him for the Son of the Most High . . . his kingdom shall never have an end."

"How can that be," replied Mary, "since I have no knowledge of man?"

"The Holy Spirit will come upon thee, and the power of the most High will overshadow thee."

"Behold the handmaid of the Lord; let it be unto me according to thy word," replied Mary.

"And with that the angel left her" (Luke i, 25-38).

Devotion to St. Gabriel seems to have begun in the 10th century. The Eastern churches celebrated his feast in December, March, November, June, and July. Since 1921 the West celebrates it on March 24th.

St. George (d. about 303)

APRIL 23RD

St. George suffered martyrdom at Lydda in Palestine shortly before the accession of the Emperor Constantine. These words contain all we know certainly of him whom the Greeks call "the great martyr" and whose devotion also spread far to the West.

Beginning with the 5th century the Christians of Syria and Egypt consecrated monasteries and churches to him. The same thing occurred a hundred years later in France and Germany. However, it was in England that St. George became and remained the most popular. In 1222, the National Council at Oxford established a holy day of obligation in his honour; in the first years at the 15th century the archbishop of Canterbury ordered that this feast be given the same solemnities as Christmas. Earlier, King Edward III had founded, in 1330, the celebrated order of the Knights of St. George also called Knights of the Garter.

Among legends relating to this martyr, the best known is that in which he worsted the dragon. This fearful animal, says the *Golden Legend*, lived in a lake near Silena in Libya. Whole armies sent against it had not been able to do away with it. Sometimes it came out of the lake, breathing fire and annihilating all that obstructed it. In the end it was appeased by being given two sheep to eat every day. When sheep were scarce, it had to be given a maiden, for whom lots were drawn. Actually the lot had fallen on the daughter of the king, when George, a military tribune, came through that country. Moved to pity, he made the sign of the cross, went off on horseback to meet the dragon which was already advancing with open mouth, and killed it at once with a blow of his lance. He then made a fine speech to this idolatrous people, after which the king and his subjects embraced the true faith and asked for baptism. The prince offered a great sum of money to the saviour of his town and of his daughter as well; but George gave it to the poor, and he went on his way, keeping nothing for himself.

St. Gertrude (d. about 1302)
NOVEMBER 15TH

St. Gertrude is one of the mystics whose works, so highly esteemed by St. Teresa and St. Francis de Sales, have always enjoyed wide appreciation. The work comprising her life and revelations is entitled *The Herald of Divine Love* and is divided into five books; the first is sort of introduction written by one of her companions; she was herself author of the second; and the three last were edited from notes made at her dictation.

The words of the mystics have a special virtue; those who have met God naturally speak about Him better than those from whom He has remained hidden. Thus it was with Gertrude to whom "heaven had accorded," as her biographer wrote, "the gift of moving hearts to their very depths and saying things so sensible, agreeable, and penetrating, that she compelled everyone to think of nothing but God, raising the most downcast souls, and adding flames to those which already possessed the fire of divine love."

It is not known who her parents were, the place or date of birth, or the year in which she died. She had been brought to the Cistercian abbey of Helfta, near Eisleben (Saxony) at the age of five. She was immediately noted for her excellent memory and extraordinary intelligence and was allowed to follow her bent for study. She learned Latin and what were then called the liberal arts. All her sisters loved her for her docile, competent, and sparkling character; all were edified by her virtues. Her fervour, however, suffered in the end from too great an application to philosophy. On January 27th, 1281, Our Lord appeared to her and reproached her with this. From then on she had no other books than the Holy Scriptures and the works of the Fathers of the Church. It was from that apparition, followed by countless others, that Gertrude dated her "conversion." Her whole life was full of ecstasies, sufferings, and heavenly communications. Sufferings and joys she received alike with gratitude and humility. "Lord," she cried, "surely the greatest of your miracles is to compel the earth to bear such a sinner as I am." St. Gertrude died one Easter Wednesday, about the age, it is believed, of forty-five.

St. Ignatius (1st century)
FEBRUARY 1ST

Under Trajan, Ignatius, Bishop of Antioch, was dragged from his episcopal throne and taken to Rome to be thrown to the wild beasts. In the course of a journey lasting many months he addressed seven letters to the churches which had shown their sympathy.

He himself tells us of his treatment. "From Syria," he writes, "by land and sea, day and night, I have already fought with beasts, chained as I was to ten leopards: I am speaking of the soldiers who guarded me—the more kindness one showed to them, the worse they became."

From Smyrna he wrote to the churches in Magnesia, Tralles, and Ephesus: "In your prayers remember me, that I may come to God; I have need of your charity and of the divine mercy, having more than ever to fear. I desire to suffer; but know not if I am worthy of it. Even though in chains, and knowing the ranks of angels and principalities, am I for that a true disciple of Christ? . . . Pray also for the Syrian Church, which has from henceforth God alone for shepherd. I salute you in the Father and in Christ Jesus, our common hope."

He was afire to shed his blood for Christ, and he begged the faithful of the Roman Church to do nothing to prevent this. "I fear that your charity may harm me . . . never will so fine an opportunity be given me to go to God, and you cannot do better than to keep quiet. The only thing I ask of you is to allow me to offer the libation of my blood to God. I am the wheat of the Lord; may I be milled by the teeth of the beasts to become the immaculate bread of Christ? Caress then, these beasts, that they may be my tomb; and let nothing be left of my body; thus my funeral will be a burden to none."

They arrived in Rome for the last day of the public games. Eighty thousand spectators crowded on to the steps of the Coliseum when Ignatius underwent martyrdom. It was brief. Two lions threw themselves upon him and devoured him in a moment, leaving on the sand only the largest of his bones.

St. Ignatius Loyola (d. 1556)
JULY 31ST

Native of the province of Guipuzocoa, in the Spanish Basque country, youngest of a noble family of twelve children, Ignatius received a military education and led, it seems, a youth that was far from edifying. Defending Pampeluna against the French, he was struck on May 20th, 1521, by a bullet which broke his leg and put his life in danger. On June 24th, at the castle of Loyola where he had been taken, the last sacraments were administered to him; then a turn for the better took place. Many months of convalescence were to follow; he asked for novels to pass the time; the only books that could be found for him were *The Golden Legend* and *The Life of Christ* by Ludolph the Carthusian. These books transformed him and he resolved to imitate the saints. After being restored to health, he pronounced the vow of chastity, hung his sword before the altar of the Virgin at Montserrat, bought a pilgrim's outfit, and prepared to depart for the Holy Land. He passed the last months of 1522 lodged in the hospital at Manresa and retiring during the daytime to a cave. From his meditations, prayers, scruples, penances, revelations, visions, graces, trials, and spiritual experiences at Manresa came the works which, together with the *Constitutions* of the Society of Jesus, have won St. Ignatius his fame as a psychologist and trainer of men. This little book, approved by Paul III in 1548, and so highly recommended by Pius XI, is entitled *The Spiritual Exercises.* After a pilgrimage to the holy places (1523), sojourns in Spain (1524-1527), in Paris (1528-1535), in Venice (1535-1537), and journeys to England, Flanders and elsewhere, Ignatius arrived in Rome about the end of 1537. He lived there until his death, directing the institution which he had formed eight years before. The Society of Jesus received the pontifical approbation by the bull *Regimini Ecclesiae militantis* of September 27th, 1540. At the founder's death it comprised twelve provinces and seventy-seven houses. Suppressed by Clement XIV in 1773, it was re-established in the kingdom of Naples in 1804 and in the entire world in 1814. Today it possesses more than five hundred universities and colleges, gives instruction to more than 200,000 pupils, and has nearly 30,000 members.

St. Jerome (d. 419)
SEPTEMBER 30TH

St. Jerome's great claim to glory is the Vulgate, or the Latin version of the Scriptures, which the Roman Church still uses today. He undertook it at the order of Pope Damasus and took thirty years to finish it. For the Psalms and the New Testament, Jerome was generally content to revise the ancient Latin translation in use in Rome at his time; the other scriptural texts he translated from the original.

Born about 347 at Strido, in Dalmatia, of a rich and Christian family, he was young when he reached Rome and followed an excellent course of classical studies. Until he received baptism in 365, his behaviour at times left something to be desired. He began to study theology at Trier; then having resolved to become a monk, he settled at Aquileia, where he lived some years in the company of Rufinus and other young clerics. From 374 to 382 we may follow Jerome to the desert of Chalcis in Syria, where he practised terrible austerities; to Antioch, where he received holy orders; to Constantinople, where he studied under Gregory of Nazianzus and worked with Gregory of Nyssa.

Returning to Rome in 382, he remained there only three years, undertaking the duties of secretary to Pope Damasus and directing a group of patrician ladies, among whom were Marcella, Paula, and Eustochium. Calumny fastened upon his relations with them: "The infamy of a false crime has been imputed to me," he wrote to them, "but it is not the judgments of men which open or shut the gates of heaven." Nevertheless, he bid the West farewell for ever, travelled in Palestine and Egypt, then went to settle in the monastery that Paula had built for him at Bethlehem. There it was that he passed his last years in study and in piety. He wrote enormously; his works take up no less than six thousand columns of Migne's *Patrology;* among them are translations of Origen, exegetical works, histories and polemic writings, several biographies, and a very extensive correspondence. As Benedict XV wrote in 1920: "The Church venerates in Jerome the greatest doctor given her by heaven for the interpretation of the Holy Scriptures."

St. Joachim (1st century)
MARCH 20TH

Nothing definite is known about the father of the Virgin Mary.

In her celebrated revelations the Venerable Maria de Agreda speaks of him in the following terms:

"St. Joachim had his family and his house at Nazareth. Illumined by heavenly light, he constantly implored God to fulfil his promises. He was humble, pure, and deeply sincere.

"For her part, Anne asked that a spouse be given her who would help her to keep the divine law. Joachim addressed the same prayer to the Lord. Their union in marriage was destined by God, and that from them should be born the mother of the Incarnate Word.

"The holy couple lived at Nazareth and kept the ways of the Lord. Each year they divided their income into three parts, offering the first to the Temple for the worship of God, distributing the second to the poor, and setting aside the third for their modest maintenance. Peace was inviolate between them; they lived in perfect conformity to custom, quietly and without quarrel. Anne submitted to the will of Joachim, who anticipated the wishes of St. Anne.

"They made a vow to the Lord that if a child were born to them, they would consecrate it to His service as a fruit of His blessing. Three years after the birth of Mary, Joachim and Anne left Nazareth and went with her to the Temple of Jerusalem. Our Queen knelt and asked their blessing, kissed their hands, and took leave of them. They returned poorer than they had come, and grieving at the loss of the rich treasure of their house, but the Lord made up for her absence, consoling them in every way.

"Six months after her entry into the Temple, our Queen learned from the Lord the day and hour of her father's death. She sent him angels from her guard to help him. They revealed to him that Mary would be the mother of the Saviour. At the same moment the holy patriarch lost his speech and, entering the way common to all men, he began his agony, struggling between the joyous news and the pains of death. He was sixty-nine and a half, and in his forty-sixth year of marriage with St. Anne; the Virgin Mary had been born to them after twenty years of marriage."

St. Joan of Arc (d. 1431)
May 30th

Born at Greux-Domremy, about 1412, to Jacques d'Arc and Isabelle Romée, Joan had one sister and three brothers. From the age of thirteen she heard voices: those of St. Michael, St. Catherine, and St. Margaret. France was then, to a large extent, in the power of the English who were in alliance with the Burgundians. In May 1428 her voices told Joan to go and find the king of France and to help him reconquer his kingdom. Her military adventure lasted fifteen months, from February 23rd, 1429, when she left Vaucouleurs, until May 23rd, 1430, when she was captured by the Burgundians at Compiègne. The twelve months which followed were those of her Calvary.

The principal dates of her glorious career are the following: March 6th, 1429, Joan was at Chinon, where she saw the dauphin; March 28th, theologians examined her at Poitiers; April 22nd, she left Blois to march upon Orléans, which the English abandoned on May 8th; on June 10th, she left for Jargeau, freed Tours, Loches, Beaugency, Patay; arrived at Auxerre July 1st; entered Troyes July 10th; was present at the king's coronation at Rheims July 17th; took Soissons July 22nd; then successively Château-Thierry, Coulommiers, Crécy, Provins; made her entry into Saint-Denis August 26th; was enobled by the king, December 29th.

On July 14th, 1430, Cauchon, bishop of Beauvais, claimed her prisoner in the name of the king of England as having been captured in his diocese. The duke of Burgundy delivered her to him for 10,000 gold francs. She was taken to Rouen, where, in obedience to England, Cauchon and about forty priests, clerks, canons, and monks condemned her to the stake. She was burned alive as a heretic and traitor, May 24th, 1431. Twenty-five years later, at the request of her mother and brothers, her trial was reviewed and she was cleared. Her beatification took place in 1909, and her canonization in 1920.

St. John the Baptist (1st century)
JUNE 24TH

The Precursor of Jesus was the son of Zachary of the order of Abia, and of Elizabeth, of the descent of Aaron. Zachary was one of the priests whose duty it was to burn incense in the temple. As he was ministering there, the angel of the Lord brought him the news that Elizabeth would give birth to a child who would be filled with the Holy Ghost from his mother's womb. But Zachary doubted the angel's word and was struck dumb until the moment when the promise was fulfilled. Meanwhile, the Virgin Mary had also learned from the archangel Gabriel that Elizabeth was going to be a mother in her old age, and she visited her relative for three months.

John the Baptist began his ministry at the age of about twenty-seven. He wore a tunic of camel's hair and a leather girdle; his food was locusts and wild honey. From Jerusalem and from all Judea people came to him to receive baptism, confessing their sins. "Brood of vipers," he said to the Pharisees, "yield the acceptable fruit of repentance . . . already the axe has been put to the root of the trees, so that every tree which does not shew good fruit will be hewn down and cast into the fire." (Matt. iii, 7-10). To the publicans he recommended not to extort from anyone; to the soldiers, to be content with their pay; to men of goodwill, to give to the poor half their food and clothing.

And above all, he announced Christ's imminent coming: "I am . . . the voice of one crying in the wilderness, Straighten out the way of the Lord. . . . I am baptizing with water; but there is one standing in your midst of whom you know nothing; he it is, who, though he comes after me takes rank before me. I am not worthy to untie the strap of his shoes." After baptizing the Saviour, John gradually sank back into obscurity. "This is the Lamb of God", he said, pointing out Jesus who was passing. "Look, this is he who takes away the sins of the world." And he later said: "This joy is mine now in full measure. He must become more and more, I must become less and less" (John i, 23-30; iii, 29-30).

John still baptized for a time at Aenon, near Salim, then his best disciples left him to follow Jesus. The last part of his life he spent as Herod's captive, chained in the prison of Machaerus, and died a victim of the vengeance of a dissolute woman. Everyone knows how Herodias had his head brought her on a dish. St. Jerome adds that for a long while Herodias savagely attacked the head of the prophet, repeatedly stabbing his tongue with a dagger.

Devotion to St. John the Baptist goes back to the 4th century. The various Christian churches have rivalled one another in showing honour and respect to him of whom Jesus said: "There is no greater . . . among all the sons of women" (Luke vii, 28), and they have set him in the front rank of the saints.

St. John the Evangelist (d. 101)
DECEMBER 27TH

A native of Galilee, John was the son of Zebedee and Salome. With his brother, James the Greater, he followed the calling of fisherman, and was among the disciples of St. John the Baptist when he was called to follow Our Lord. Jesus had a predilection for him; he was "the disciple whom Jesus loved" (John xxi, 7), as the Gospel sometimes describes him. At the Last Supper, he was seen leaning his head against the breast of the Master who was about to die. It was to him that Jesus, at the point of death, confided the Virgin Mary, and he took her into his house; finally it was he who, the first of the apostles with St. Peter, ran to the tomb which Magdalen had found empty, and who first of them all recognized the risen Saviour on the shores of the lake of Tiberias.

However, he had not always been perfect. "Master," he said one day, "we saw a man who does not follow in our company casting out devils in thy name, and we forbade him to do it. But Jesus said, Forbid him no more; the man who is not against you is on your side." And later when some Samaritans having shut their door against the Saviour, James and John said to him: "Lord, wouldst thou have us bid fire come down from heaven, and consume them? But he turned and rebuked them, You do not understand, he said, what spirit it is you share. The Son of Man has come to save men's lives, not to destroy them" (Luke ix, 49-56). Another time, the two brothers asked for themselves the first places in the kingdom of heaven. "Master, we would have thee grant the request we are to make. And he asked them, What would you have me do for you? They said to him, Grant that one of us may take his place on thy right and the other on thy left, when thou art glorified," which offended the other apostles, and led Jesus to say, "Whoever has a mind to be first among you, must be your slave" (Mark x, 35-44).

The Acts show us Peter and John remaining united in friendship after Pentecost; together they went up to the temple to pray; together they preached and were thrown into prison; both were sent together to Samaria there to bring down the Holy Ghost upon the newly baptized.

At the end of the 1st century, St. John was bishop of Ephesus. There it was, according to tradition, that he died, aged over a hundred. Tradition also adds that he was plunged into boiling oil during a voyage to Rome and was later exiled to the island of Patmos.

St. Joseph (1st century)
MARCH 19TH

The Gospel, sole source of information concerning the life of St. Joseph, tells us that the foster father of Jesus was an upstanding man, a scion of the house of David who practised the trade of carpenter at Nazareth.

Betrothed to the Virgin Mary, "he was for sending her away in secret . . . when an angel of the Lord appeared to him in a dream, and said, Joseph, son of David, do not be afraid to take thy wife Mary to thyself, for it is by the power of the Holy Ghost that she has conceived this child; and she will bear a son, whom thou shalt call Jesus, for he is to save his people from their sins . . . And Joseph awoke from sleep, and did as the angel of the Lord had bidden him, taking

40

his wife to himself; and he had not known her when she bore a son, her first-born, to whom he gave the name Jesus" (Matt. i, 19-25).

"Because there was no room for them in the inn," Mary and Joseph had taken refuge in a cave which served as shelter for men and beasts. It was there that the Virgin "brought forth a son . . . whom she wrapped in his swaddling-clothes, and laid in a manger. . . . And so (the shepherds) found Mary and Joseph there, with the child lying in the manger" (Luke ii, 7-17).

The wise men came in their turn to adore Jesus. "As soon as they had gone, an angel of the Lord appeared to Joseph in a dream, and said, Rise up, take with thee the child and his mother, and flee to Egypt; there remain, until I give thee word. For Herod will soon be making search for the child, to destroy him." After Herod's death, the angel reappeared to Joseph to enjoin him to leave Egypt. "So he arose, and took the child and his mother with him, and came into the land of Israel . . . and settled down in a city called Nazareth" (Matt. ii, 13-23).

When Jesus was presented in the temple, St. Luke notes: "The father and mother of the child were still wondering over all that was said of him"; and he adds that "every year, his parents used to go up to Jerusalem at the paschal feast". In the course of one of these journeys, Jesus, aged twelve, parted company with his parents. "It was only after three days that they found him. He was sitting in the temple, in the midst of those who taught there. . . . His mother said to him, My Son, why hast thou treated us so? Think, what anguish of mind thy father and I have endured, searching for thee." Jesus replied: "Could you not tell that I must needs be in the place which belongs to my Father? . . . but he went down with them on their journey to Nazareth, and lived there in subjection to them" (Luke ii, 33-51).

After which, the Gospels make no further mention of him who

was worthy to be the foster father of Our Lord and the spouse of the Immaculate Virgin. Without doubt, he died before the Saviour's Passion, for, says St. Francis de Sales, it would have been unthinkable that Jesus on the Cross could have commended his mother to St. John, if Joseph had still been there to care for her.

St. Lucy (d. 303?)
DECEMBER 13TH

St. Lucy, patroness of Syracuse, is supposed to have suffered martyrdom in that city during Diocletian's persecution. Certain painters show her in the company of Sts. Thecla, Barbara, Agatha, Agnes, and Catherine. Like these, Lucy had vowed her virginity to God. She was clever enough to put off for three years the nobleman who wished to marry her. Other painters have represented her as kneeling before a tomb or yoked to a pair of oxen, sometimes also with her neck pierced by a dagger. These pictures recall episodes in her biography, true or legendary. It is said that, to avenge himself for being refused, her suitor denounced her as a Christian as she was on her way back from praying for the conversion of her mother at the tomb of St. Agnes. Upon her refusal to apostasize, she was condemned to a house of ill fame. But it proved impossible to make her leave the tribunal; an invincible force kept her rooted to the spot. Even a yoke of oxen was unable to drag her thence. To get rid of her it was necessary to light a pyre in the pretorium and, as she remained alive in the midst of the flames, for an executioner to pierce her throat with his dagger.

St. Luke (1st century)
OCTOBER 18TH

Disciple, helper, and friend of St. Paul, "beloved Luke, the physician' (Col. iv, 14), is the only one of the evangelists who was not a Jew. A native of Antioch, he belonged to the Hellenic world; his mother tongue was Greek, and he used it with an elegant simplicity.

He never saw Our Lord in the flesh, but he may have been, before his conversion, one of those pagans who mixed with the Jews of the Dispersion, professing monotheism as they did, and with them frequenting the synagogue on the Sabbath day.

Did he embrace Christianity about the year 42, when Paul and Barnabas came to preach at Antioch; or was it even some years earlier when, after the stoning of St. Stephen, the Judo-Christians fled from Jerusalem to settle in the Syrian metropolis?

The fact is that about the year 50 he appeared at the side of St. Paul at Troas. He reached Macedonia with him and accompanied him as far as Philippi. It appears he remained there for some time, leaving the apostle to continue his journey alone. Paul found him there again on his return through Macedonia. Luke then accompanied him to Jerusalem from whence Paul, arrested in the Temple, was taken captive to Caesarea. He did not leave him at all between 57 and 59, the two years this captivity lasted.

When the apostle appealed to the tribunal of the Emperor Nero and was taken, escorted by soldiers, to Rome, Luke embarked in his company and was shipwrecked with him on the Maltese coast. Nothing is known of his last years, or when he died. It is only known that he never left his master during the latter's captivity in Rome which ended in martyrdom in 67.

St. Luke is the author of the Acts of the Apostles and of the third Gospel. He alone has preserved for us the parables of the lost sheep and the prodigal son, of the Pharisee and the publican, of Dives and Lazarus. He alone has recorded Jesus' words: "If great sins have been forgiven her, she has also greatly loved" (Luke viii, 47); the prayer of the Crucified for his executioners; and the promise to the good thief: "This day thou shalt be with me in Paradise" (Luke xxiii, 43). It is this which has made Dante call him "historian of the compassion of Christ."

St. Mark the Evangelist (1st century)
APRIL 25TH

St. Mark the Evangelist is generally identified with the person called in Acts and Epistles sometimes John, by his Jewish name, sometimes Mark, by his Greco-Roman name.

He was a cousin of St. Barnabas and a native of Jerusalem, where his mother Mary lived in a big house which served as meeting-place for the first Christian community. St. Peter went there directly on leaving the dungeon where Herod Agrippa had imprisoned him. Rhoda, a young servant, came to let him in, and the apostle found numerous persons at prayer (Acts xii, 12). It was doubtless he who baptized Mark, since he calls him his "son" (I Pet. v, 13).

In the same year 44, St. Paul and St. Barnabas arrived at Jerusalem, bringing help for the Christians who were in distress because of famine. When they left again for Antioch, Mark joined them, and accompanied them to Cyprus and to the coast of Asia Minor. At Perge in Pamphylia he left them, and while they entered the defiles of the Taurus to reach the high plateau of Pisidia and Lycaonia, he returned to Jerusalem. His conduct displeased Paul and caused the difference he later had with Barnabas.

When, in the year 50, the two apostles were deliberating over a visit to the churches founded by them on their first voyage, Barnabas wished to take Mark with them; Paul opposed it, so that each went his way, Paul taking Silas and the road to Cilicia, while Barnabas sailed for Cyprus with his cousin Mark. St. Paul nevertheless bore no grudge against St. Mark, for some ten years later we find them together in Rome, and shortly before his martyrdom the apostle sent word to Mark to leave the East and return to him.

Mark was also the collaborator of St. Peter and had from him, it is believed, the facts and incidents from which he composed his Gospel. An ancient tradition makes Mark the founder of the church of Alexandria; another, more recent, affirms that he suffered martyrdom under Trajan.

St. Martha (1st century)
JULY 29TH

Sister of Lazarus and Mary of Bethany *(See July 22nd)*, St. Martha is known to us only by the Holy Scripture; in it three references are made to her.

The first is on the occasion of the repast she prepared for Jesus; on that day Our Lord addressed the following words to the too-restless mistress of the house: "Martha, Martha, how many cares and troubles thou hast! But only one thing is necessary; and Mary has chosen for herself the best part of all, that which shall never be taken away from her" (Luke x, 41-42).

Martha appears a second time after the resurrection of Lazarus. "Jesus," says St. John, "loved Martha, and her sister, and Lazarus." Learning that Jesus was come, Martha said to Him: "If thou hadst been here, my brother would not have died; and I know well that even now God will grant whatever thou wilt ask of him." Jesus said to her: "Thy brother will rise again." Martha said to Him: "I know well enough that he will rise again at the resurrection, when the last day comes." Jesus said to her: "I am the resurrection and life; he who believes in me, though he is dead, will live on, and whoever has life, and has faith in me, to all eternity cannot die. Dost thou believe this?" She answered Him: "Yes, Lord, I have learned to believe that thou art the Christ; thou art the Son of the living God; it is for thy coming the world has waited" (John xi, 1-28).

Finally, Martha is referred to by the evangelist when he tells of the meal of which Jesus partook at the house of Simon the Leper. He simply tells us, this time, that Martha took care of the service (John xii, 1-9).

Relics of St. Martha are believed to have been found at Tarascon in 1187. In the following century, the Franciscans assigned her feast a date in their breviary, and from that time her cult took on a certain importance in the West. Hotelkeepers have chosen her as their patroness.

St. Martin of Tours (d. 397)
NOVEMBER 11TH

Born at Sabaria in Pannonia about 325, Martin was enrolled at fifteen in the imperial horse guards. It was at Amiens, where he was on garrison duty, that he divided his cloak with a stroke of his sword to clothe a poor man. Shortly afterwards, at about twenty, he was baptized, left the army, and was made an exorcist by St. Hilary at Poitiers.

Warned in a dream of the approaching death of his parents, Martin returned to his own far-off country where he had the happiness of converting his mother. While on the road returning to Gaul, a rumour reached him that the bishop of Poitiers had been exiled. He then withdrew to the island of Gallinaria and lived there as a solitary until the day when he heard that St. Hilary had been set at liberty. After stopping in Rome, he again arrived in Poitou and there led for ten years the cenobitic life according to the rule of St. Basil. Thus came to be founded Ligugé, the most ancient monastery in the West.

In 371, the people of Tours, seeking a bishop, carried off Martin by force and took him to their town. His episcopate lasted for twenty-six years, during which he converted not only Touraine but also Berry, Anjou, Beauce, Paris, Trier, Luxemburg, Sennonais, and even far-off Dauphiny. He travelled light, always followed by a party of monks, sometimes riding on a donkey, ordinarily on foot or by boat; praying, preaching, accomplishing many miracles and good works; converting families, villages, whole tribes; casting down temples and idols, raising monasteries and churches in their place; consolidating

47

his gains, and everywhere leaving monks or priests to carry on his work.

In 397 he collapsed from exhaustion at Candes. As his disciples begged him not to leave them, the old man began to weep and said: "If God finds that I can still be of use to his people, I do not at all refuse to work and to suffer longer." He died with his face turned to the window to see the sky, and at once became the most popular saint of the West. In France, four thousand churches are dedicated to him and more than five hundred villages bear his name.

St. Mary Magdalen (1st century)
JULY 22ND

Devotion to St. Mary Magdalen has been widespread in the West since the 11th century. Few historians still defend the story of her sojourn in Provence, but the exegetes continue to question whether what the Gospels say of Mary of Bethany and of the harlot who anointed Our Lord must be applied to her. This is the problem and how it has been resolved:

The Gospel three times mentions Mary, sister of Martha and Lazarus, who lived at Bethany in Judea. In St. Luke she is seen sitting at the Saviour's feet, while the busy Martha reproaches her for not bothering about the meal. "Martha, Martha," said Jesus, "how many cares and troubles thou hast! But only one thing is necessary; and Mary has chosen for herself the best part of all, that which shall never be taken away from her" (Luke x, 41-42). Mary of Bethany reappears throughout the chapter in which the resurrection of Lazarus is recounted (John xi); she is finally found with Martha and Lazarus at a repast which Simon the leper offered to Our Lord. That day she poured a pound of spikenard on the head and feet of the Saviour. "Why should not this ointment have been sold?" said Judas. "It would have fetched two hundred silver pieces, and alms might have been given to the poor." "Why do you vex the woman?" said Jesus. "You have the poor among you always; I am not always among you" (Mark xiv, Matt. xxvi, John xii).

Elsewhere the Gospel mentions, without giving her a name, a harlot who, at the house of Simon the Pharisee, came to kneel before Our Lord, anointing His feet with perfume, covering them with kisses and tears, and drying them with her hair. To the scandalized Pharisees, Jesus declared: "If great sins have been forgiven her, she has also greatly loved," and He sent away the harlot saying: "Thy faith has saved thee; go in peace" (Luke vii).

Finally the Gospel tells us of a woman called Mary Magdalen or Mary of Magdala in Judaea. She was of those women whom Jesus had delivered from evil spirits and who now were following Him and assisting Him with their goods. She was "the woman out of whom he had cast seven devils," which does not necessarily mean that she was or had been a sinner, since diabolical possession does not in any way imply a state of sin. We find Mary Magdalen again at Calvary, watching from afar; she was present at the burial, coming back to the sepulchre on Sunday before dawn; she was the first witness of the resurrection; it was she whom Jesus charged to announce His resurrection to the disciples. "Jesus said to her, Mary. And she turned and said to him, Rabboni (which is the Hebrew for Master)." Jesus added, "Do not cling to me thus; I have not yet gone up to my Father's side. Return to my brethren, and tell them this; I am going up to him who is my Father and your Father, who is my God and your God" (Matt. xxviii, Mark xvi, Luke xxiv, John xx).

What can be concluded from these texts? Must we see, with the Eastern liturgists and a number of Western exegetes, three different people in these women to whom Our Lord showed so much goodness? In this case, Mary Magdalen would not necessarily be a former sinner. Must we see one and the same person? Or must we see two, distinguishing on one hand Mary of Bethany, and on the other hand identifying Mary of Magdala with the anonymous sinner of St. Luke? In the last two cases, Mary Magdalen would certainly be such as she is represented in popular belief—the woman to whom many faults had been forgiven before she entered so intimately into the Saviour's circle.

St. Matthew (1st century)
SEPTEMBER 21ST

As was customary among the Jews, Matthew, son of Alphaeus, had two names; he was also called Levi. He was a publican or collector of taxes at Capharnaum, not far from the frontier separating the lands of Herod Antipas from those of his brother Philip. His profession was one of the least honourable; everyone considered all tax collectors and their masters to be more or less robbers, and the Pharisees treated them as public sinners. It was as direct a challenge to public opinion for the Saviour to associate Matthew the publican with His apostolate as it was later for Him to visit Zaccheus, another member of this despised profession.

The Gospel tells that, after having healed a paralytic, "As he passed further on his way, Jesus saw a man called Matthew sitting at work in the customs-house, and said to him, Follow me; and Matthew rose from his place and followed him. And afterwards, when he was sitting at table in the house, many publicans and sinners were to be found sitting down with him and his disciples. The Pharisees saw this, and asked his disciples, How comes it that your master eats with publicans and sinners? Jesus heard it, and said, It is not those that are in health that have need of the physician, it is those who are sick. Go home and find out what the words mean. It is mercy that wins favour with me, not sacrifice. I have come to call sinners, not the just" (Matt. ix, 9-13).

From that moment, Matthew withdraws into the apostolic college and no longer calls attention to himself. With the other apostles, he witnessed the ascension and was in the upper room on the day of Pentecost. Transformed by the Holy Ghost, he, like his colleagues, became a herald of the Christian message; then, having spread it for a long time by word of mouth—for perhaps some twenty years—he wrote it down. He did this in Aramaic, in the language which had supplanted Hebrew and which Jesus spoke. This Aramaic version addressed to the Palestinian Jews has not been preserved; we possess only its translation into Greek made towards the end of the 1st century; it is this, placed first among our Sacred Scriptures, which we call "The Gospel according to St. Matthew." The writers of Christian antiquity are not in agreement as to which country was the scene of the apostolate of the first of the evangelists, nor as to the date of his death.

St. Michael the Archangel
SEPTEMBER 29TH

St. Michael is, with St. Gabriel and St. Raphael, one of the three archangels mentioned in Holy Scripture. There he appears as prince of the celestial hierarchy, protecting the chosen people and achieving the downfall of the infernal powers. The primitive Church considered him also the defender of Christians and their consolation in trials. Still today the liturgical prayers show him charged with the guidance of souls here below, to protect them from the devil's snares and to lead them to the light eternal: *signifer Sanctus Michael repraesentet eas in lucem sanctam.*

From the earliest Christian times St. Michael was the object of a cult. In Phrygia, near Hierapolis, he took the place of the god of the thermal waters; here and there in Gaul he turned Mercury out of the high places; in Germany he sometimes was substituted for Wotan on the banks of the Rhine. A church dedicated to him was built near Constantinople as early as the 4th century.

On May 8th, 492, the archangel appeared on the summit of Mount Gargano, and the cave where he had appeared became the most frequented place of pilgrimage in southern Italy. The Lombards chose him as their patron, struck coins in his image, and consecrated to him their most beautiful temples. A hundred years later, when the plague was raging at Rome, Pope Gregory the Great saw him in a vision sheathing his flaming sword to signify that he would put an end to the scourge. A cryptiform church was built about 608 on Hadrian's mausoleum in gratitude to the archangel for this good office.

Doubtless still more famous than the Roman and Apulian sanctuaries is the one dedicated on a Norman hill in 709, called Mont-Saint-Michel. The archangel, it was said, had appeared to St. Aubert, bishop of Avranches, expressing his wish to be honoured by the Gauls. From that moment, devotion to St. Michael took on a new impetus; it travelled to the east with the Celtic monks, who carried it as far as the Bavarian Alps, from whence it spread throughout the West.

St. Monica (333-387)
MAY 4TH

She was born at Tagaste, now Souk-Ahras, in the department of Constantine. Her parents, small landed proprietors, brought her up a Christian, and married her to a pagan older than herself, named Patricius. He was a man of spirit but irascible and debauched, by whose violence and infidelity she suffered a great deal. She also had to put up with the caprices of an ill-disposed mother-in-law. It was through prayer and her daily attendance at Mass that she found patience and gentleness. She herself used to say to women who complained of being unhappy at home: "If you can master your tongue, not only do you run less risk of being beaten, but perhaps you may even, one day, make your husband better." For her part she quickly tamed her mother-in-law; as for Patricius, she ended by loving him and, after thirty years, by converting him.

She had three children, of whom one was the future St. Augustine. He was first her pride because of the success he achieved in his studies and as a teacher; then he was her sorrow through his conduct. It is known that he lived for ten years with a mistress and was a Manichean. Hoping that discussions would convert her son, Monica urged a certain bishop to debate with him, but the prelate considered him too presumptuous and too good a disputant to let himself be convinced: "Content yourself with praying for him," he replied to the mother. She returned to the charge weeping, and he sent her away saying: "Go. Continue as you have done till now; it is impossible that the son of so many tears should perish." She followed this counsel, and Augustine was touched by the grace of God when he was twenty-eight.

Widowed, Monica rejoined him in Italy. It was a question which, mother or son, would advance the most rapidly in holiness. However, Monica aspired to see God, and to leave this world. "What am I still doing down here?" she said to her son. She died at Ostia as they were both to re-embark for Africa, she being fifty-six and St. Augustine thirty-three.

St. Nicholas (d. 324)
DECEMBER 6TH

Few saints enjoy such great popularity and few are credited with so many miracles. Sts. John Chrysostom, Peter Damian, and Bonaventure have vied in eloquence with one another in telling of the merits and the goodness of St. Nicholas. Born at Patara in Lycia, he visited the Thebaid, ruled a great monastery, was imprisoned for a time for his faith, and ended his life as archbishop of Myra.

It is doubtless the story of his restoring life to the children put in the salting tub which caused him to become the patron and the annual benefactor of school children. St. Bonaventure tells the story in a sermon. St. Nicholas was, it seems, on his way to the Council of Nicaea, when he entered an inn whose owner, not content with having killed two young boys for the sake of their meagre purse, had cut them up and was about to sell them piecemeal to his clients. The bishop restored them to life and then converted this murderer.

Another famous tale is that of the three marriageable girls who did not succeed in getting married. Poor and not knowing what to do with them, their father was about to put them into a house of ill fame. Nicholas took advantage of the fact that this odious man slept with his window open, to go one night and throw a purse filled with gold into his room. A few days later, the eldest daughter was married. In the same way, Nicholas delivered to the second the dowry she needed. Soon she, too, found a husband. The saint was discovered at the moment when he was throwing up from the street the purse destined for the third. The father, who had been hiding in the shadow, recognized him; he fell at his feet, weeping in penitence and gratitude, and from then on did not cease to sing his praises everywhere.

St. Patrick (d. about 461)
MARCH 17TH

Ireland, Scotland, and Wales compete for the honour of having given birth to St. Patrick. His father, the deacon Calpurnius, had a farm beside the sea. About 404 it was pillaged by pirates who carried off Patrick, aged sixteen. They sold him to an islander who employed him for six years in tending his flocks, after which Patrick fled and returned to his parents.

In a dream he had a vision that caused him to devote himself to the evangelization of Ireland, still in idolatry. He crossed the sea, stayed with the monks of Lérins, then went to Auxerre where, from 415 to 432, he was at the school of the bishops St. Amator and St. Germain. It is thought that the first conferred the diaconate on him, and the second consecrated him bishop.

Recently freed from Roman domination, the Irish were then ruled by a host of minor kings. It was principally towards these personages that Patrick directed his zeal on arriving in the country. Wielding absolute power, their religion was their subjects'; monopolizing the land, they alone controlled the right to authorize the building of churches. The story of the evangelization of Ireland is almost entirely written in terms of the conversions made by St. Patrick among the heads of the clans and their families.

Many legends have been added to these accounts, such as the "Purgatory" of St. Patrick; and also the "Promises" which God made to him before his death. The Purgatory of St. Patrick is a great subterranean cave, situated on an island of Lough Dergh in Ulster, where the saint used to go to meditate on the judgment of God and to give himself up to penances. Since his death it has always been a place of pilgrimage, and certain souls have thought it sufficient to pass some time there to avoid the sufferings of purgatory in the world to come. As for the famous Promises, there is one which assures the Irish that they will be judged by St. Patrick on the last day.

At any rate, these legends express the extreme veneration of the Irish people for the apostle who made them Christian.

St. Paul (d. 67)
JUNE 30TH

Born at Tarsus in Cilicia, in the first decade of our era, St. Paul belonged to an important and devout family of Jews. He possessed the status of a Roman citizen by birth. He received the Hebrew name of Saul, which he later Latinized to Paulus. He spoke Aramaic and Greek. At the school of the Rabbi Gamaliel of Jerusalem, he studied exegesis, Jewish dogma, traditional law and casuistry, and became a model Pharisee.

In the eyes of enlightened Jews an inglorious Messias did not make sense. To worship the Crucified of Calvary was to betray the religious

56

ideal of Israel and the very reason for her existence. Paul persecuted the Christians with a sort of rage until the day when the risen Christ appeared to him and transformed him. From that moment he was wholly devoted to spreading the knowledge and love of Our Lord.

During the years following his baptism we find him preaching at Damascus and "in Arabia"; twice making the journey to Jerusalem; staying at Caesarea, at Tarsus, at Antioch in Syria. From 45 to 48 he was at Cyprus, in Pamphylia, in Pisidia, and in Lycaonia. In 49, he conferred with St. Peter and St. James at Jerusalem. From 50 to 52, he journeyed through Phrygia, Galatia, Macedonia; preached at Philippi, Thessalonica, Beroea, and Athens; stayed many months in Corinth, and returned to Antioch, having passed through Caesarea and Jerusalem. In the spring of 53, Paul again departed for Ephesus; then he visited all the churches in Macedonia, went to Achaia, passed the winter of 57-58 at Corinth, stayed in the Aegean Islands and in the ports of the Asiatic coast, and returned to Jerusalem for Pentecost in the year 58. There the Jews attempted to kill him; they succeeded only in having him arrested by the Roman authorities who kept him captive at Caesarea for two years. As he had appealed to Caesar, in the end they sent him to Rome, where, after two more years of captivity, he was set free in the spring of 63.

It is known that the apostle again visited Crete, Ephesus, Troas, Macedonia, and Epirus; perhaps he also stayed for a short time in Spain. It was in Asia, apparently, that the police of Nero arrested him; and it was at Rome that, after renewed imprisonment, he was beheaded. According to Eusebius his martyrdom took place in 67, three years after that of St. Peter.

St. Peter (d. 64)
JUNE 29TH

Simon lived in Bethsaida on the north shore of the lake of Tiberias and there followed the calling of fisherman with his father, Jona, and his brother, Andrew. He married and for some time was a disciple of St. John the Baptist. When, having left all, he came to join the Saviour, "Jesus looked at him closely, and said, Thou art Simon, the son of Jona; thou shalt be called Cephas (which means the same as Peter)" (John i, 42). He at once took his place at the head of the apostolic college; from that time he appeared in all the Gospel scenes and almost always played the leading part in them.

He was present at the marriage at Cana, at the feeding of the five thousand, at the miraculous draught of fishes, at the cure of his mother-in-law and of a host of other sick people. With James and John, the sons of Zebedee, he witnessed the Transfiguration on Thabor and the Agony in the Garden. He heard, and sometimes provoked, the most important statements of the divine Master. Before anyone, he professed belief in the divinity of the Saviour: "Thou art the Christ, the Son of the living God." Jesus then replied: "Blessed art thou, Simon son of Jona; it is not flesh and blood, it is my Father in heaven that has revealed this to thee." Then he added: "And I tell thee this in my turn, that thou art Peter, and it is upon this rock that I will build my church: and the gates of hell shall not prevail against it" (Matt. xvi, 16-18).

During the passion, Peter also showed his courage in striking Malchus with a sword, but he ended by abandoning his Master and even denied Him thrice in the high priest's courtyard. He was the first of

58

the apostles to see Jesus risen and, after the ascension, took leadership of the little Christian community. On the day of Pentecost, he spoke in the name of all and converted three thousand people. His authority constantly grew; miracles took place along his way; his shadow, cast upon the sick, sufficed to cure them.

About the year 43, Peter was at Jerusalem where Herod Agrippa had him imprisoned; he was there again about the year 50, presiding over the council and deciding, with Paul and Barnabas, on the entry of the Gentiles into the Church. He had first established his episcopal see at Antioch; it is believed that he occupied it for seven years and gave place, about 42, to St. Evodius. He stayed afterwards at Corinth; then was bishop of Rome, where he died, crucified head downwards, during Nero's persecutions.

St. Peter of Alcántara (1499-1562)
OCTOBER 19TH

Born at Alcántara of a noble family, Peter Garavito was educated at Salamanca and entered the Franciscans of Manxarretes at sixteen. He preached in Spain and Portugal for a score of years, fulfilled the duties of provincial and commissioner general of his order, and died at the monastery of Arenas in 1562. He is one of the great Spanish mystics of the 16th century, and one who carried austerity to a superhuman degree.

He declared to St. Teresa that he had lived three years in a monastery without lifting his eyes, only knowing his brethren by their voices; he always went barefoot without sandals; only ate every other day and, further, sprinkled his food with ashes; only slept for two hours a night, squatting or kneeling against the wall. Even in agony and consumed with fever, he refused a glass of water offered him, gasping: "Jesus was willing to thirst on the cross!" When they told him he was going to die, he murmured: *"Laetatus sum in his quae dicta sunt mihi.* I rejoice when they say unto me, I will go up into the house of the Lord." After his death, appearing to St. Teresa in glory, he said to her: "Blessed be that penance which has brought such a reward."

The celebrated Carmelite venerated him as her outstanding benefactor; it was he in fact who came to her rescue when all opposed or abandoned her. Having passed through the same mystical states, he alone understood and reassured her; and, in the face of all opposition, declared his conviction that God had destined her to reform Carmel.

Peter of Alcántara instituted a severe reform in his order known as the Alcantarine, from which arose a galaxy of saints. He wrote a *Treatise on Mental Prayer,* which St. Teresa, Louis of Granada, and St. Francis de Sales considered a masterpiece. Pope Gregory XV declared that he found in it "a shining light to lead souls to heaven and a doctrine prompted by the Holy Spirit"; and when he beatified its author in 1623 he accorded him the title of "doctor of mystical theology."

St. Philip Neri (1515-1595)
MAY 26TH

His father was a notary in Florence who devoted himself to alchemy. His mother died prematurely, but she was replaced by an excellent stepmother, and Philip's childhood was happy and pure. He was born poet, musician, psychologist, and non-conformist. He was quick to seize the pleasing side of things and showed in everything an attractive freedom and originality of spirit.

When he was seventeen his father persuaded him to visit an uncle from whom he had expectations, who had a business at San Germano at the foot of Mounte Cassino. Philip set out, but arriving at his destination, he neglected his business and expectations and devoted himself to piety under the guidance of a Benedictine from the nearby monastery.

Three years later, about 1536, he arrived in Rome. It appears that he lodged there for fourteen years with his compatriot, Galeotto Caccia, director of pontifical taxes. He gave lessons to the sons of his host, studied theology with the Augustinians and spent late nights in the churches and the catacombs, preached in the streets, visited the hospitals and slums, converted rich and poor, made friends among the intelligentsia, and became affiliated with the confraternity of the "Oratory," whose name was soon to serve to desginate his own work and his congregation.

This was formed between 1551, when Philip entered the priesthood, and 1572, when we find him at the head of an important group, including specifically Tarugi, later archbishop of Avignon, and Baronius, author of the *Annales Ecclesiastici*. It received its definitive approval in the bull of July 15th, 1575, spread to Naples in 1585, and later to France.

Philip Neri was one of the most popular saints, everyone loved and venerated him. God gave him a foretaste of celestial happiness during his lifetime. "Enough, Lord, enough!" he often said. "Hold back, I implore, the floods of Your Grace." Or again, "Withdraw Thyself, Lord, I am but a mortal; I cannot bear so much joy." He was also heard to declare that "for one who truly loves God, there is nothing more difficult and painful than to remain alive."

St. Raphael the Archangel
OCTOBER 24TH

St. Raphael is one of the three archangels mentioned by Holy Scripture and honoured by the Roman liturgy, the two others being St. Gabriel and St. Michael.

All we know of him is revealed by the Book of Tobias. Tobias was about to depart for Media in order to recover a sum of money lent by his father to Gabelus. Raphael appeared in the form of a beautiful youth in order to accompany him and, during the journey, was a constant source of benefaction to him.

On the banks of the Tigris he saved Tobias from a sea monster who was about to devour him. A little farther on he urged him to visit Raguel, whose demoniacal daughter brought death to all who married her. "He has a daughter called Sara, and neither chick nor child besides," said Raphael to Tobias. "Of all he possesses thou mayest be heir, if thou wilt claim his daughter's hand in marriage, thou hast but to ask him, and she is thine." As he hesitated, the angel added: "Heed me well ... and thou shalt hear why the fiend has power to hurt some and not others. The fiend has power over such as go about their mating with all thought of God shut out of their hearts and minds wholly intent on their lust, as if they were horse or mule, brutes without reason" (Tob. vii, 11-17).

The marriage was celebrated and the first three days were devoted to prayer. "The evil spirit fled; it was overtaken by the angel Raphael and in the waste lands of Upper Egypt, and there held prisoner" (Tob. viii, 3-4). Then, while the wedding feast continued, Raphael alone went to Gabelus, who discharged his debt. Returning to find Tobias, he led him and his wife home.

Before returning to heaven, he restored sight to Tobias' father. "Prayer fasting, and alms, said he, here is better treasure to lay up than any store of gold . . . When thou, Tobias, wert praying, and with tears . . . I, all the while, was offering that prayer of thine to the Lord. Then, because thou hadst won his favour, needs must that trials should come, and test thy worth. And now, for thy healing, for the deliverance of thy son's wife Sara from the fiend's attack, he has chosen me for his messenger. Who am I? I am the angel Raphael, and my place is among those seven who stand in the presence of the Lord. . . . I was at your side, eating and drinking, but only in outward show; the food, the drink I live by, man's eyes cannot see. And now the time has come when I must go back to him who sent me; give thanks to God and tell the story of his great deeds" (Tob. xii, 8-21).

St. Scholastica (d. 543)
February 10th

Twin sister of St. Benedict, Scholastica was born, about 480, into a rich family at Norcia in Umbria. The mother of these children died in bringing them into the world. They loved one another tenderly and were brought up together until the age of fourteen, when Benedict left for Rome in order to pursue his studies there.

It is thought that Scholastica followed her brother when he became a monk and that, having become a nun, she settled in the valley of the Liris at the foot of Monte Cassino. Benedict directed her as he did other nuns placed under his guidance. He saw his sister once a year. On the appointed day Scholastica went to Monte Cassino; Benedict came to meet her; they passed some hours together in a guest-house of the abbey, and ate together, then each went his way.

Their last interview is reported by St. Gregory the Great. They were at table and the time was approaching for them to separate, when Scholastica said to her brother: "Don't let us part yet, but let us wait until morning."

"What are you thinking of, my sister? Not for the world would I pass a night outside the monastery."

Scholastica wept a moment in silence, then, inclining her head, hid her face in her hands. No sooner had she uncovered it than a crash of thunder shook the house to its foundations. The peaceful sky became black, flashes of lightning rent the night, the heaven opened its floodgates, the wind blew, and a tempest threatened to carry everything before it. "May God forgive you, but what have you done, my sister?" said Benedict.

"I asked you and you would not listen to me; so I have asked God, who has heard me, for I see indeed that you will not return to the monastery this evening."

They passed the night in pious conversation and parted at dawn, never to see one another again. Three days later, as he was at the window of his cell, St. Benedict saw the soul of his sister rising to heaven in the form of a dove. He gave thanks to God, sent for her body and had it placed in his own tomb, not wishing that death should separate them.

St. Sebastian (d. 288)
JANUARY 20TH

A native of Milan, Sebastian set out for Rome and enlisted in the army, not that he had any definite inclination for a career of arms, but he wished to be of use to the persecuted Christians without arousing too much suspicion.

The first to benefit from his devotion were the brothers Marcus and Marcellinus, recently condemned to death. At the request of their parents, a respite of three days had been granted to allow them to reflect and possibly to apostasize. Sebastian went to the house of Nicostratus, clerk to the prefecture, who, with the help of the jailer Claudius, was charged with their surveillance. Before them all he spoke so wondrously of Christ that not only the parents of the condemned but also the clerk Nicostratus, the jailer Claudius, and sixteen prisoners confided to their guard asked to be baptized. These conversions also led to that of Agrestius Chromatius, governor of Rome, who released the converted prisoners. Sebastian, for his part, continued to show himself such a good soldier that Diocletian named him captain of the Pretorian guard.

Nevertheless, a recrudescence of persecution took place in 286, and several of those mentioned above were victims: Nicostratus and his wife were drowned in the Tiber, Marcus and Marcellinus were shot with arrows, and the son of Chromatius was beheaded. These events provided the centurion with many new opportunities to exercise his zeal.

But finally his role was discovered. Diocletian reproached him with ingratitude. Vainly did Sebastian protest that he had always meticulously fulfilled his military duties; the emperor delivered him to the archers, who, having shot him through with arrows, left him for dead. However, he recovered from his wounds, and was urged to hide himself. But burning to be martyred in his turn, Sebastian deliberately set himself in Diocletian's path and said to him: "Know that you will have no peace until you cease from shedding innocent blood!" Overcome with surprise and rage, the emperor ordered him to be cudgelled to death and his body thrown into the sewer.

St. Simeon Stylites (d. 459)
JANUARY 5TH

Stylites comes from a Greek word, *stulos*, signifying column. It was in fact upon a column that St. Simeon passed the greater part of his strange existence.

He was born on the borders of Cilicia and Syria; at the age of thirteen he was watching his father's sheep when he heard this verse of the Gospel: "Woe upon you who laugh now; you shall mourn and weep" (Luke vi, 25). He asked an old man the meaning of these words, and it was explained to him that eternal happiness is obtained by suffering, and that it is in solitude it is most surely gained.

The young boy at once joined some hermits of the district, with whom he lived for two years. Then he lived for some ten years at the monastery of Teleda where his unusual mortifications finally caused his dismissal. Then, reaching Tellnesin, near Antioch, he settled in a cell where they walled up the door on Ash Wednesday and in which he remained confined until Easter morning without food.

Importuned by increasingly indiscreet visitors and admirers, Simeon resolved to escape their importunities by living thenceforth on a column. He stood upright, without shelter, exposed to the intemperate climate, almost continually absorbed in prayer. On feast days, after nones, he addressed two exhortations to the people, and at all times replied in a friendly way to those who had recourse to his arbitration and advice. Numerous were the spiritual and bodily cures which he accomplished. Moreover, homage meant nothing to him, and he remained perfectly humble.

He died in 459 in his sixty-ninth year, as he was bowing in beginning his first prayer. There are still remains, at Gata'at Sema'an, of the immense basilica raised upon his place of penance.

Sts. Simon and Jude (1st century)
OCTOBER 28TH

The feasts of St. Simon and St. Jude are doubtless celebrated together because, in enumerating the apostles, the writers of the synoptic Gospels place them one after the other.

The first is surnamed by them "Quanana" or "the zealous," as much to distinguish him from Simon Peter as to mark the zeal which he put at God's service. The second was really called Judas, but we call him rather Jude, in order to distinguish him from his namesake, the traitor, Judas Iscariot. This is also why St. Luke calls him "Judas, son of James," and why St. Mark designates him by his surname "Thaddeus" or "man with the strong chest."

At the Last Supper, Jude interrupted Jesus to ask Him a question which, however, received no reply. "Lord," said St. Jude, "how comes it that thou wilt only reveal thyself to us, and not to the world?" (John xiv, 22-23). "This question," writes Bossuet, "arose naturally from the talk which had preceded it because there we have seen that the Saviour had declared he would manifest himself by the Holy Spirit to his friends and not to the world. Here then is the great secret of divine predestination. St. Jude went at once to the great mystery: How is it? What have we done that we have merited more than others? Should we have believed, if you had not given us faith? Should we have chosen you, if you had not first chosen us?

" 'Why, Lord, why?' said St. Jude. Jesus alone could resolve this question; but he kept the secret . . . He did not answer it; and without even appearing to hear, he again repeated: 'If a man has any love for me, he will be true to my word; and then he will win my Father's love, and we will both come to him, and make our continual abode with him' (John xiv, 23-24). As though he had said: 'O, Jude, ask not what it is not given to you to know; do not seek the cause of the preference, adore my counsels; all that concerns you in this is that you keep my commandments; all the rest is my Father's secret, the unfathomable secret the Sovereign reserves to himself' " *(Meditations on the Gospel,* ninety-second day).

According to a certain tradition, Jude and Simon evangelized Persia and were martyred there. The first is invoked in desperate cases; the second has been taken as patron by curriers and pit sawyers.

St. Stephen (d. 33)
DECEMBER 26TH

St. Stephen is called "the first martyr"; it was he, indeed, who first shed his blood for the faith. The Acts of the Apostles relate that he was "full of grace and power, performed great miracles and signs among the people." He belonged, it seems, to that group of Hellenized Jews who had lost the use of Hebrew because they remained abroad after the Babylonian captivity. He had become a Christian, had been ordained deacon by the apostles, and as such was given the care of feeding the poor and the widows to whose support the Christian community in Jerusalem was committed.

"There were those who came forward to debate with him, some of the synagogue . . . but they were no match for Stephen's wisdom, and for the Spirit which then gave utterance. Thereupon they employed agents to say they had heard him speaking blasphemously of Moses, and of God. Having thus roused the feelings of the people, and of the elders and scribes, they set upon him and carried him off, and so brought him before the Council. There they put forward false witnesses, who declared, 'This man is never tired of uttering insults against the holy place, and the law. We have heard him say that the Nazarene, Jesus, will destroy this place, and will alter the traditions which Moses handed down to us.' "

The High Priest asked him if this were true. Then, in a long speech recorded in the *Acts*, Stephen showed them that this Jesus of Nazareth was indeed the Messias announced by Moses and the prophets, and come on earth to call all men to salvation.

"At hearing this, they were cut to the heart, and began to gnash their teeth at him. But he, full of the Holy Spirit, fastened his eyes on heaven, and saw there the glory of God, and Jesus standing at God's right hand; I see heaven opening, he said, and the Son of Man standing at the right hand of God. Then they cried aloud, and put their fingers into their ears; with one accord they fell upon him, thrust him out of the city, and stoned him. . . . Thus they stoned Stephen; he, meanwhile, was praying; Lord Jesus, he said, receive my spirit; and then, kneeling down, he cried aloud, Lord, do not count this sin against them. And with that, he fell asleep in the Lord. . . . Stephen was buried by devout men, who mourned greatly over him" (Acts vi-viii).

St. Teresa of Avila (1515-1582)
OCTOBER 15TH

St. Teresa was born at Avila of a noble family, on March 28th, 1515. Her parents brought nine children into the world; her father, Alonzo Sanchez de Cepeda, had three by a first marriage. Teresa was in her twelfth year when she lost her mother. At the age of seven she ran away to join the Moors who, she thought, would consent to cut off her head. Cheated of martyrdom, for a time she imitated the anchorites by building hermitages in a garden. Then these holy aspirations were counteracted by what she later called her great sins, that is to say; reading novels, flirtations, and frivolous chatter.

At sixteen she was boarded at an Augustinian convent in her native town and remained there eighteen months. She then spent a few days at the house of an uncle whose pious conversation caused her to become a nun.

At the Carmel of Avila, where she took her vows in 1534, the nuns could receive visits in the parlour and even in their cells. For some twenty years Teresa tried to enjoy both the delights of prayer and the pleasures of secular conversation. Very unhappy, she finally understood that she owed God the gift of her whole self. From that time her life consisted in prayer, apparitions of Christ, sufferings, and ecstasies.

In 1562 Teresa set about the reform of the Carmelite order. At the cost of innumerable persecutions and difficulties, she established poor and austere convents at Avila, Toledo, Valladolid, Salamanca, Alba, and elsewhere. At Toledo she had only three ducats to begin her buildings. "Teresa and three ducats," she said, "are nothing; but

God, Teresa, and three ducats are sufficient to make a success of everything." St. John of the Cross and Father Jerome Gratian helped her extend her reform to all branches of the Carmelite order.

St. Teresa is one of the most universally admired of women. Her intelligence and charm, her chivalrous spirit, her talent as a writer, and her experience of supernatural ways have won a privileged place for her among the saints of the Church. She died in ecstasy at the convent of Alba, her head supported by Mother Anne of St. Bartholomew, her eyes fixed on the crucifix, on the night of October 4th-5th, 1582.

St. Theresa of the Child Jesus (1873-1897)
OCTOBER 3RD

Of a merchant family, St. Thérèse de l'Enfant Jesus was born at Alençon on January 2nd, 1873. Louis Martin and Zélie Guérin, her parents, had in their youth wished to embrace the religious state. Of their nine children, only five daughters survived, all of whom became nuns.

Theresa, the youngest, showed astonishing spiritual precocity. At two, she had the instinct of prayer; at three she was making sacrifices; at five she was able to profit by sermons. She lost her mother when four and a half, and two years later had a prophetic vision of the illness of which her father was to die. From October 1881 to December 1885, Theresa was brought up by the Benedictines of Lisieux; from March to May 1883 she suffered from a strange malady, characterized by violent crises, extended delirium, and prolonged fainting spells.

Her entry into the convent of the Carmelites of Lisieux took place on April 9th, 1888. Before pronouncing her vows she declared she "was come to Carmel to save souls and to pray for priests." After having worked in the laundry, the refectory, at the turning-box, and in the sacristy, she was made, in February 1893, assistant to the novice mistress. Out of obedience she adorned the chapel of her convent with paintings, and occasionally composed a few verses.

Nothing then appeared extraordinary in this life which was known later to have been filled with suffering and heroism. The young nun followed what Fenelon had once called the "way of childhood." "I prefer," she wrote, "the monotony of obscure sacrifice to all ecstasies. To pick up a pin for love can convert a soul." More even than scorn, she sought oblivion. In December 1894 she began her autobiography, entitled *The Story of a Soul*, which has spread the world over.

On April 3rd, 1896, Theresa began to cough blood. From that time on, enduring a true spirtual martyrdom, she seemed deprived of the light of faith and the sweetness of hope and speedily declined. On September 30th, 1897, at five o'clock in the afternoon, her last agony began. Shortly after seven she was heard to murmur: "I would not suffer less." Then she added: "I love Thee, my God," and drew her last breath. A short time before, she had written: "I want to spend my heaven doing good on earth."

St. Thomas (1st century)
DECEMBER 21ST

The only evangelist who speaks of St. Thomas specifically is St. John. He mentions him three times.

The first time is when Lazarus was raised from the dead. Learning that Jesus wished to go to Bethany, in that part of Judaea where He had just escaped from His enemies, the disciples said to Him: "Master, the Jews were but now threatening to stone thee; art thou for Judaea again?" Jesus replied: "Come, let us make our way to him. Thereupon Thomas, who is also called Didymus, said to his fellow-disicples, Let us go too, and be killed along with Him" (John xi, 8-16).

In the long farewell address which He made to them before going to His death, Jesus promised His own to return one day to fetch them: "There are many dwelling-places in my Father's house; otherwise, should I have said to you, I am going away to prepare a home for you? And though I do go away, to prepare you a home, I am coming back; and then I will take you to myself, so that you too may be where I am. And now you know where it is I am going; and you know the way there. Thomas said to him, But, Lord, we do not know where thou art going; how are we to know the way there? Jesus said to him, I am the way; I am truth and life; nobody can come to the Father, except through me." (John xiv, 2-6).

On the occasion of one of the apparitions of the risen Jesus to His apostles, "Thomas was not with them when Jesus came. And when the other disciples told him, We have seen the Lord, he said to them, Until I have seen the mark of the nails on his hands, until I have put my finger into the mark of the nails, and put my hand into his side, you will never make me believe. So, eight days afterwards, once more the disciples were within, and Thomas was with them; and the doors were locked. Jesus came and stood there in their midst; Peace be upon you, he said. Then he said to Thomas, Let me have thy finger; see, here are my hands. Let me have thy hand; put it into my side. Cease thy doubting, and believe. Thomas answered, Thou art my Lord and my God. And Jesus said to him, Thou hast learned to believe, Thomas, because thou hast seen me. Blessed are those who have not seen, and yet have learned to believe" (John xx, 24-29).

A tradition has it that after Pentecost, St. Thomas went to evangelize the Parthians, Medes, and Persians, and that he penetrated as far as India and was martyred at Calamine. He is sometimes represented with a square rule in his hand, and both architects and masons have chosen him as their patron. His apocryphal *Acts* relate that during the course of his travels he laid out for Guaduphara, king of India, a magnificent palace of a peculiar type, the plan of which no architect of the country had been able to draw.

St. Thomas Becket (1117-1170)
DECEMBER 29TH

In 1155, Henry II, king of England and of a part of France, took as his chancellor Thomas Becket, archdeacon of Canterbury. This prelate, of Norman origin and possessor of an immense fortune, was considered one of the most capable men of his age. Some have compared him with Richelieu, whom he resembled by his statesmanlike qualities and his love of pomp. The visit which he paid, in 1158, to Louis VII, king of France, long remained famous. Thomas Becket crossed the Channel with six frigates and two thousand men. On his way to Paris, he traversed the cities preceded by two hundred and fifty musicians, surrounded by his many greyhounds, followed by eight carriages each pulled by six horses. Then came carts bearing his bedroom, his kitchen, his chapel, and his silver; then, on high chargers, hundreds of horsemen composed of the flower of the nobility, bedecked with gold and silver.

When the episcopal see of Canterbury fell vacant, Henry II gave it to his chancellor. Thomas was ordained priest, June 1st, 1162, and consecrated bishop two days later; after this he became the second person in the kingdom; and after this, too, he changed his life entirely and became the most austere of prelates.

Persuaded that the office of prime minister and that of chief of the Church in England were not reconcilable, he had resigned his functions as chancellor, to the king's annoyance. Henry II was still more displeased with him when, in 1164, on the occasion of the "Councils" of Clarendon and of Northampton, the archbishop took the pope's part against him. Thomas had to flee, disguised as a lay brother, and sought refuge at Compiègne with Louis VII. Then he stayed at the abbey of Pontigny and at that of St. Columba, near Sens. Four years passed at the end of which, upon the request of the pope and of the king of France, Henry II finally gave permission to Thomas to return to England. He counted thenceforward on a blind submission from him, but he was quickly disabused when he discovered that the archbishop continued to defend the prerogatives of the Roman Church against the royal pretensions. "Cursed be they that eat my bread unless they deliver me from this insolent priest," he cried one day. Some courtiers took upon themselves to carry out this cruel wish. Thomas, who was expecting to be killed, wished to be immolated in his cathedral, and it was there, on the night of December 28th, 1170, that he was cut down and hacked to death with swords.

St. Thomas More (1478-1535)
JULY 9TH

A good example of an "honest man" and Christian humourist, this great humanist, a friend of Erasmus and Holbein, refused to recognize his sovereign as spiritual head of the Angelican Church and died with a heroism full of good humour and simplicity. He wished to be helped up on to the scaffold ("I can manage to get down alone"); protested his fidelity to God and to the King; recited the *Miserere;* embraced his executioner and gave him a piece of gold ("Courage, my good man, don't be afraid; but take care, for I have a short neck and you have to look to your honour"); bandaged his eyes himself, put out of the way his beard, which, in his opinion, "did not deserve to be cut off since it had betrayed nothing"; put his head on the block; and the executioner cut it off with a blow of his axe.

St. Timothy
JANUARY 24TH

There is no one to whom Paul gave higher praise than to Timothy. He was born in Lycaonia, of a Greek father and a Jewish mother named Eunice. When Paul came to Lystra for the first time, he converted Eunice and doubtless baptized her son too. On returning, he found Timothy grown so virtuous, courageous, and selfless that he made him his close companion and lifelong friend.

From the spring of the year 50 to the fall of the year 52, the latter accompanied his master to Ephesus, to Jerusalem, and to Rome; with him he traversed Phrygia, Galatia, and Macedonia; he also assisted him in evangelizing the Thessalonians and Corinthians. In the beginning of the year 53, Timothy was at Ephesus with Paul, when the latter entrusted him with a mission to the churches of Macedonia and Corinth. We know that on this occasion the Corinthians did not give a warm welcome to the missionary. In the years following, we find him at Paul's side in Macedonia, in the Peloponnesos and at Troas. It seems that he rejoined him at Rome between 61 and 63.

Twice St. Paul wrote to him during his second captivity in Rome.

We know the moving phrases in which he took leave of him: "I have fought the good fight; I have finished the race; I have redeemed my pledge; I look forward to the prize that is waiting for me, the prize I have earned. The Lord, that judge whose award never goes amiss, will grant it to me when that day comes" (II Tim. iv, 7-8).

It is believed that Timothy survived his master by some thirty years, presiding as bishop over the destinies of the church of Ephesus. He was, it is said, stoned to death during a pagan feast which he was trying to prevent his flock from attending.

St. Valentine (d. about 270)
FEBRUARY 14TH

Today is celebrated the feast of two saints named Valentine whose rather similar stories have not been entirely clarified.

The first was a priest in Rome said to have been arrested under Claudius the Goth. Appearing before the emperor, he openly confessed his faith, and when questioned by him about Jupiter and Mercury, declared that they were shameless and contemptible characters. He was then committed to a magistrate named Asterius, who had an adopted daughter who was blind. Valentine cured her and converted at the same time Asterius and his family. Learning this, the emperor had him beaten and later decapitated on the Flaminian Way. In the 4th century, Pope Julius I built a church in honour of this martyr; in the 7th century, Pope Honorius I restored it and it became a very popular centre of pilgrimage.

The other St. Valentine is reputed to have occupied the see of Terni in Umbria in the year 223. Informed of his virtues and miracles, a Roman philosopher named Crato begged him to come and cure his son, stricken by an incurable malady. The bishop went to Rome and promised to do what was asked if the father and his family would be converted. The condition was accepted and fulfilled, and even three young Athenians, disciples of Crato, renounced the gods to embrace Christianity. On his side, Valentine worked the cure he promised.

As soon as the prefect Abundius learned what had happened, he had the bishop beheaded. His body was then taken back to Terni by the converted Athenians, and St. Valentine is still honoured as patron of that city.

In medieval days it was believed that birds began to pair on February 14th, whence the origin of the custom of sending "Valentines".

St. Vincent (d. 304)
JANUARY 22ND

This martyr is one of the most universally honoured of the Latin Chruch. He was born at Huesca and had been ordained deacon by Valerius, bishop of Saragossa, who, old and tongue-tied, could not preach. Vincent substituted for him in his preaching ministry.

These duties brought him into the limelight; and he was among the first to be arrested, with his bishop, when the persecutuions of Diocletian began. They took him in chains to Valencia to appear before Dacian, governor of the province. He interrogated Valerius, endeavouring to intimidate him. The old man expressed himself with difficulty and at one moment stopped short.

Dacian was already triumphant, seeing in his silence the promise of apostasy. But Vincent, for whom it was simply the usual effect of the prelate's infirmity, asked to speak for him. "My son," replied the bishop, "I commit to you the charge of testifying to our faith as you have that of preaching the Gospel." Then Vincent protested eloquently that nothing whatsoever should triumph over their common fidelity to Christ.

Furious at this interference, Dacian momentarily forgot about the bishop and had the deacon put to torture. The latter seemed to think nothing of it. Dacian ordered that his flesh be torn with iron hooks, that he should be roasted over a slow fire, and he urged the torturers to redouble their savagery. It was of no avail; the victim was only the more firm and joyful in confessing his faith. The governor thought that he would finally give signs of weakness or at least die in fearful anguish. But here again his hope was in vain, for his victim prayed and sang psalms until the end, and it was in the full joy of the spirit that he drew his last breath.

St. Vincent is here and there taken as patron by the wine-growers, but unless we accept that it is because of a pun on the first syllable of his name, the reason for this patronage is unknown.

St. Vincent de Paul (d. 1660)
JULY 19TH

Born at Pouy in the Landes, about 1580, Vincent de Paul was the third child of a family of labourers comprising four sons and two daughters. He seems to have received at birth those qualities which characterize the best of the French peasantry: good sense and perspicacity, tenacity, some ambition, a happy facility for expressing ideas clearly, and the faculty of adapting himself to men and circumstances. After having tended sheep, he was sent to the college of the Grey Friars of Dax; then his father sold two oxen to pay for his theological studies at the Unviersity of Toulouse.

Ordained priest in 1600, Vincent opened a school at Buzet, tried without success to obtain a good ecclesiastical benefice, and went as far as Marseilles to collect three hundred crowns due to him. Taking sail to return to Narbonne, he was captured by Corsairs who led him captive to Tunis. Nevertheless, he managed to escape and returned to France. In 1610 we find him in Paris, almoner of Queen Margot, first wife of Henry IV. The king had received him on his return from captivity, as he carried a secret message from the court of Rome, and became his protector. Vincent was made pastor of Clichy in 1611, became a tutor in the Gondi family in 1613, obtained various advantageous benefices; then suddenly, in 1617, he resigned all honours and from that time his behaviour became that of a saint.

Apart from some months passed as a country priest at Châtillon (Doubs) in 1617, and numerous journeys throughout France, it was at Paris that he lived from that time until his death. Made almoner of the galleys in 1619, in 1625 he founded the congregation of Priests of the Mission or Lazarists, to evangelize the poor of the countryside; this name of Lazarist came to them from the priory of St. Lazarus where they were established. In 1634, Monsieur Vincent, as he was called, founded the congregation of Sisters of Charity, as we have told on March 15th, on the occasion of the feast of St. Louise de Marillac. To him is also due the charity for the care of foundlings, established with the idea of collecting infants abandoned at street corners or on the church porches. It is scarcely an exaggeration to say that his influence extended to all religious France of his day.

It is, however, as a man of heart and a friend of the disinherited that his name has come down to posterity. He did so much for the poor, the sick and for children, that his name is still known and respected everywhere. Since his day it is less easy than before to pass for a Christian without showing an interest in the unfortunate and doing works of charity.

List of Saints Specially Invoked

St. Acacius is said to cure headaches (May 8th).

St. Adam has been taken as patron by gardeners (December 19th).

St. Agatha, patroness of nurses, is invoked against breast diseases and against fire (February 5th).

St. Agia is invoked in lawsuits (April 18th).

St. Albert the Great was given as patron by Pius XII, in 1941, to students of natural sciences (November 15th).

St. Aloysius Gonzaga, named as patron of youth by Pius XI in 1926 (June 21st).

St. Alphonsus Liguori. Pius XII has given him as patron to confessors and professors of moral theology (August 2nd).

St. Ambrose is the protector of bees and domestic animals (December 7th).

St. Andrew Avellino is one of the patrons of a holy death, and is also invoked against sudden death (November 10th).

St. Andrew the Apostle, patron of fishermen and fish dealers, is also invoked by women who wish to become mothers (November 30th).

St. Anne is the patroness of old-clothes dealers, of seamstresses, laceworkers, housekeepers, of carpenters, turners, cabinetmakers, stablemen, and broommakers. She is also invoked against poverty and to find lost objects (July 26th).

The Annunciation of the Blessed Virgin is the feast of news dealers and ribbonmakers (March 25th).

St. Anthony of Padua is invoked for the protection of asses and horses, and specially to find lost objects (June 13th).

St. Apollonia is invoked against toothache (February 9th).

The Assumption of the Blessed Virgin is the feast of harnessmakers and fish dealers (August 15th).

St. Balbina is invoked against scrofulous diseases (March 31st).

St. Balthasar, patron of manufacturers of playing cards and sawmen, is also invoked against epilepsy (January 11th).

St. Barbara, patroness of firemen, mathematicians, fireworks makers, artillery men, architects, smelters, saltpetre workers, brewers, armourers, hatters, tilers, masons, miners, and carpenters, is also invoked against lightning, sudden death, and final impenitence (December 4th).

St. Bartholomew is the patron of butchers, tanners, and bookbinders (August 24th).

St. Benedict is invoked against temptations of the devil, inflammatory diseases, erysipelas, fever, and kidney disease (March 21st).

St. Bernard of Menthon was named patron of mountain climbers by Pius XI in 1923 (May 28th).

St. Blaise, patron of woolweavers and carvers, builders and stonecutters, is also invoked against wild beasts, coughs, whooping cough, goitre, and throat diseases in general (February 3rd).

St. Brice is invoked against diseases of the stomach (November 13th).

St. Camillus de Lellis was named by Leo XIII, in 1886, as patron of the sick and of infirmarians (July 18th).

St. Catherine of Alexandria is the patroness of philosophers, old maids, scholars, knife grinders, millers, wheelwrights, tanners, turners, and spinners (November 25th).

St. Catherine of Bologna is the patroness of painters (March 9th).

St. Catherine of Siena was given as patroness to the nurses of Italy by Pius XII in 1943 (April 30th).

St. Catherine of Sweden is invoked against miscarriages in childbirth (March 24).

St. Cecilia is the patroness of musicians and makers of musical instruments (November 22nd).

St. Christopher, patron of archers, market carriers, fullers, fruit dealers, and automobilists, is invoked against sudden death, storms, hail, toothache, and impenitence at death (July 25th).

St. Clare is the patroness of embroidery workers, of gilders, and of washerwomen. She is invoked against diseases of the eye and for good weather (August 12th).

St. Claudius is the patron of turners and toymakers (June 6th).

St. Clement of Rome is the patron of boatmen; he is also prayed to for the cure of sick children (November 23rd).

St. Concordia is the patroness of nursing mothers and children's nurses (August 13th).

St. Cosmas is the patron of doctors, surgeons, druggists, and midwives (September 27th).

Sts. Crispin and Crispinian are the patrons of shoemakers, glove makers, and weavers (October 25th).

St. Cuthbert, patron in England of shepherds and mariners (March 20th).

St. Cyriacus is invoked against diseases of the eye (August 8th).

St. Dionysius the Areopagite is invoked against headaches and against the devil (October 9th).

St. Dominic of Sora is invoked against fever and snakes (January 22nd).

St. Dympna is prayed to for those who are insane or possessed by the devil (May 15th).

St. Eligius or Eloi is the patron of metalworkers, blacksmiths, wheel-wrights, veterinarians, saddlers, cutlers, miners, locksmiths, clock-makers, carriage makers, toolmakers, cab drivers, farmers, jockeys, farm workers, and labourers. He is also invoked for the cure of sick horses (December 1st).

St. Emidius is invoked against earthquakes (August 5th).

St. Erasmus, patron of navigators, is invoked against storms, against colic, intestinal diseases of children, and during the pains of child-birth (June 2nd).

St. Eulogius, patron of carpenters (March 11th).

St. Eustachius is considered efficacious in fighting fires and protect-ing us from the fires of eternity (September 20th).

St. Felicitas of Rome is prayed to for male children (July 10th).

St. Felix of Nola is invoked against perjury (January 14th).

St. Fiacre is the patron of gardeners, pewterers, boxmakers, hosiers, and tilemakers (August 30th).

St. Florian is invoked against fire (May 4th).

The Four Crowned Martyrs have been taken as patrons by masons, sculptors, and stoneworkers (November 8th).

St. Francis Borgia is prayed to against earthquakes (October 10th).

St. Francis de Sales was given as patron to writers by Pius XI in 1923 (January 29th).

St. Francis Xavier is invoked against plague. In 1904 Pius X named him patron of the Propagation of the Faith and other similar works (December 3rd).

St. Genesius of Rome, patron of clowns and comedians (August 25th).

St. Genevieve is invoked against fever (January 3rd).

St. George is invoked against skin diseases (April 23rd).

St. Gertrude of Nivelles is invoked against fever, against mice and rats, especially field rats, for cats, and to obtain good lodgings when travelling (March 17th).

St. Giles or Egidius, patron of cripples and spur makers, is invoked against cancer, sterility in women, the terrors of the night, and madness (September 1st).

St. Gomer is invoked against hernia. He is the patron of woodcutters, turners, glovemakers, cowherds, and those unhappily married (October 11th).

St. Gregory the Great is the patron of singers and scholars (March 12th).

St. Guy or Vitus is invoked for dogs and against rabies, also against sleeping sickness, epilepsy, and the dance which bears his name (June 15th)

St. Hilary is invoked against snakes (January 14th).

The Holy Innocents are the patrons of choirboys and foundlings (December 28th).

St. Honoré, patron of bakers (May 16th).

St. Hubert is the patron of hunters, foresters, smelters, furriers, and makers of precision instruments. He is invoked against rabies and for the protection of dogs. (November 3rd).

St. Hugh of Cluny is invoked against fever (April 29th).

St. Ignatius Loyola was named by Pius XI, in 1922, patron of those making the Spiritual Exercises (July 31st).

The Immaculate Conception was given as patroness to the soldiers of the United States by Pius XII in 1942 (December 8th). This date is also the feast of tapestry workers and upholsterers, clothworkers, and coopers.

St. Irene, patroness of young girls (June 28th).

St. Isidore, patron of labourers (May 10th).

St. Ives is the patron of lawyers, jurists, advocates, notaries, bailiffs, and orphans (May 19th).

St. Jean Baptiste de la Salle. Pope Pius XII has given him as patron to the educators of youth (May 15th).

St. Jean Marie Vianney was named by Pius XI, in 1929, patron of parish priests (August 9th).

St. Jerome is the patron of students (September 30th).

St. Jerome Emiliani, named as patron of orphans by Pius XI in 1928 (July 20th).

St. John Chrysostom is invoked against epilepsy. In 1908 Pius X named him patron of preachers (January 27th).

St. John of God named as patron of the sick and the dying by Leo XIII (March 8th).

St. John of Nepomucene is invoked for the protection of bridges; against indiscretions and calumnies; in order to make a good confession (May 16th).

St. John the Baptist, patron of bird dealers, of cutters and tailors, is also invoked against spasms, convulsions, epilepsy, hail; also prayed to for the protection of lambs (June 24th).

St. John the Evangelist is the patron of theologians. He is invoked against burns and poisons, and also for good friendships (December 27th).

St. Joseph, patron of carpenters, wheelwrights, cabinetmakers, and of a good death. He was given as patron to the universal Church by Pius IX in 1870, as patron of workmen by Benedict XV in 1920, as patron of those who combat atheistic Communism by Pius XI in 1937 (March 19th).

St. Julian is the patron of fiddlers, jugglers, clowns, shepherds, pil-

grims, hotelkeepers, ferrymen, and travellers seeking good lodging
(February 12th)

St. Lawrence is specially invoked against lumbago and fire, and for
the protection of vineyards. He is also the patron of cooks and restaurateurs (August 10th).

St. Leonard is invoked at childbirth. He is the patron of prisoners, of
coppersmiths, blacksmiths, locksmiths, porters, coal miners, and in
certain places, of greengrocers and coopers (November 6th).

St. Louis is the patron of builders, of button makers, embroidery
workers and haberdashers, of distillers, hairdressers, and barbers
(August 25th).

St. Lucy is invoked against eye diseases, dysentery, and in general
against hemorrahages (December 13th).

St. Luke is the patron of doctors, painters, glassmakers, lacemakers,
of artists in general, and particularly those who use colour and
brush (October 18th).

St. Margaret cures kidney diseases and comes to the aid of those in
childbirth (July 20th).

St. Mark, patron of glaziers and lawyers, is particularly invoked
against scrofulous diseases and final impenitence (April 25th).

St. Martha, patroness of innkeepers, hotelkeepers, and laundresses
(July 29th).

St. Martin, patron of horsemen and tailors, is specially invoked for
the protection of geese (November 11th).

Blessed Martin de Porres is the patron of mulattoes and is invoked
against rats (November 3rd).

St. Mary Magdalen, patroness of perfumers, tanners, glovemakers,
and repentant women and girls (July 22nd).

St. Mary of Egypt is also the patroness of women who have formerly lived in sin (April 2nd).

St. Matthais, patron of carpenters, tailors, and repentant drunkards, is particularly invoked against smallpox (February 24th).

St. Maurice is the patron of dyers and is invoked against gout (September 22nd).

St. Michael, patron of coopers, hatmakers, swordsmen, haberdahsers, and grocers, is often invoked for a good death. Pius XII named him as patron of policemen in 1950 (September 29th).

The Nativity of the Blessed Virgin is the feast of drapers and needle makers, fish dealers, distillers, coffeehouse keepers, cooks and restaurateurs, tilemakers and potters, pinmakers and workers in silk, gold, or silver (September 8th).

St. Nicholas, patron of scholars, boatmen, fishermen, dock workmen and sailors, coopers and brewers, travellers and pilgrims and those who have unjustly lost a lawsuit; also invoked against robbers (December 6th).

St. Nicholas of Tolentino is particularly invoked for the souls in purgatory (September 10th).

St. Odo is prayed to for rain (November 18th).

Our Lady of Loreto was named patron of aviators in 1920 by the Congregation of Rites (December 10th).

St. Pantaleon is one of the patrons of doctors and is invoked against consumption (July 27th).

St. Pascal Baylon was given as patron by Leo XIII, in 1897, to Eucharistic congresses and organizations (May 17th).

St. Paul, patron of ropemakers, is invoked against hail and serpent bite (June 30th).

St. Peter is the patron of locksmiths and cobblers; in parts of France he is also the patron of harvesters; he is also prayed to for the success of affairs before the Roman court (June 29th).

St. Peter Claver was named by Leo XIII, in 1896, as patron of negro missions (September 9th).

St. Quentin is invoked against coughs (October 31st).

St. Quirinus or Cyrinus is invoked against evil spirits, in cases of possession or obsession (March 25th).

St. Raymond Nonnatus, patron of midwives, is invoked for women at childbirth and for little children (August 31st).

St. Roch, patron of tilemakers and surgeons; he is invoked against plague, ills of the knees, and cattle diseases (August 16th).

St. Romanus is prayed to for madmen and those who have been drowned (February 28th).

St. Scholastica is invoked against storms (Febrary 10th).

St. Sebaldus is invoked against the cold (August 19th).

St. Servatus is invoked against rats, mice, diseases of the legs, and in general for the success of enterprises (May 13th).

St. Severus, patron of drapers, wool manufacturers, weavers, and silk makers (February 1st).

St. Simon, patron of curriers (October 28th).

St. Stephen is patron of smelters and stonecutters (December 26th).

St. Suitbert is invoked against throat troubles (April 30th).

St. Theresa of the Child Jesus was named patroness of the missions by Pius XI in 1923 (October 3rd).

St. Thiemo, patron of engravers (September 28th).

St. Thomas Aquinas was given as patron by Leo XIII, in 1880, to Catholic schools (March 7th).

The Transfiguration of Our Lord is in certain countries the feast of pork butchers and cleaners (August 6th).

St. Ursula, patroness of the educators of young girls, is invoked for a good death (October 21st).

St. Vaast or Gaston is invoked for children who are late in learning to walk (February 6th).

St. Valentine, patron of engaged couples and those who wish to marry, is specially invoked against epilepsy, plague, and fainting diseases (February 14th).

St. Véran is invoked for the help of those who are insane (September 11th).

St. Victor, patron of cabinetmakers, is invoked against lightning (July 21st).

St. Vincent, patron of winegrowers (January 22nd).

St. Vincent Ferrer, patron of makers of tile and brick, pavement workers, and plumbers (April 5th).

St. Willibrord is invoked against epilepsy and convulsions (November 7th).

St. Wolfgang, patron of carpenters, is also invoked against paralysis and apoplexy (June 7th).

St. Zita, patroness of maidservants and housekeepers (April 27th).